RED BLOOD GIRL

Book 1 of the *Blood Girl* series

K.A.BARRON

This is a work of fiction. Names, characters, organizations, places, events, and incidents are either products of the author's imagination or are used fictitiously.

Published by Kevin Barron

www.kabarron.com

ISBN 978-1-99-117530-4 (ePub)

ISBN 978-1-99-117531-1 (Softcover)

Contents

Your free book is waiting

Pressed back into service as a fighter pilot when war breaks out, the man Mouse knows as Grandad meets a young girl in the rubble of a ruined city. It is a meeting which will change his life. And the lives of others he has yet to meet.

First Blood Girl provides context and insight to the unfolding story in the *Blood Girl* series.

Get a free digital copy of the prequel story *First Blood Girl* by tapping the image of the book above or on this sentence.

If you're reading a hard copy book with pages, you can use this link online: https://bit.ly/first-blood-girl

[Before]

WE'D BEEN AVOIDING THE COPS all day, so at first I was real wary when the old man walked into the disused warehouse where we were hiding out. We'd only arrived that morning and had been tired after being on the move for half the night, so I hadn't had time to set up any sensors.

The other kids saw him first. I had my back to him, so the first I knew was when Casey and Smit suddenly jumped to their feet. He had come in from the street and was picking his way through the empty racks scattered about the large room in dimming light.

"It's okay," he said, holding out a hand to us half dozen kids. "I'm not with the cops."

That was obvious really. He was way too old. Even at twelve I could tell he was older than most adults. That also meant that he was probably a blueblood. They live longer.

"What do you want?" said Casey. He was the biggest of us at fourteen. His hand was gripping a piece of wood with nails in it. I'd seen him use it too: on some other vagrant who'd tried to steal food from us. He was the leader of our gang, even when Boris was around.

"I don't want any trouble," said the old man. "I just want someone to help me."

"What kind of help?" I asked.

"Shush Mouse! Don't talk to him," said Pip. He was even smaller than me and scared of everything.

I ignored Pip and got to my feet and walked over to the old man. I stood looking up at him, trying my best to look defiant and faintly dangerous. Of course he didn't look at all intimidated. On the other hand, I noticed he had kind, blue eyes.

"What's your name?" he asked.

"Don't tell him!" said Pip.

"Mouse," I said.

He looked me up and down.

"Suits you," he said.

It's not my real name of course. They call me that because my family name is Muswell and it sounds a bit similar. And because I'm small. Always have been. They said it was because my mother smoked when she was pregnant with me. My real name is Deanna, which I never liked, so I was pleased to leave it behind.

"How old are you?"

I was expecting Pip to call out again, but he didn't. None of them spoke. They could see I'd taken control of the situation.

"Thirteen," I said, trying to stand taller so I actually looked it.

He nodded and smiled, then he held out his hand.

"Come along," he said as if he believed the lie about my age, which I'm sure he didn't. "I've got a little job for you."

I should have asked him what the job was, but I didn't want to put him off by seeming to be fussy about what I did. I could always leave if I didn't like it.

There was something about him I liked, but you don't live vagrant for three years and trust everyone just like that, especially not a blue-blood. So I looked at him, trying to work him out.

"You do a good job at this, there might be more," he said. "You'd like that wouldn't you?"

What vagrant wouldn't? We were quite illegal of course. If a redblood doesn't have a job, then they're a vagrant and can be rounded up by the police and set to work in the factories, the labor camps or out in the farm towns. The vagrants they round up end up doing the worst jobs and it's hard to move out of them to become a regular redblood with a proper job. A lot of the vagrants are kids. I reckoned it's because their parents die of the blood sickness.

Vagrants are the lowest of the low as far as bluebloods are concerned. Even some of the redbloods look down on us. I've always thought that was particularly unfair. Bluebloods may see us as inferior, but we don't want our own thinking that.

Then Boris came in carrying a plastic bag containing the result of his scavenging.

Boris was the only adult in our gang. He was a big gentle guy who was surprised when anyone liked him. He had been a tech, but had lost his job when his factory burned down. They said it was terrorist action and blamed the Rads. That never made sense to me. Why would redbloods want to hurt other redbloods? Because it was the redbloods who suffered when things like that happened. I bet the blueblood owners weren't out of pocket for long; just the insurers.

But it meant I got Boris. I got a sense he was the kind of guy adults made fun of. Casey was defensive when he first met him, but he warmed to him. We kids liked him because he listened to us and only showed us stuff if we were interested. Most adults try to tell you things whether you're interested or not.

On the street, I started out just scavenging food and finding things I could sell on as best I could. Then I started tinkering with technology. I'd find things that people had thrown out. I started putting them together to see what would happen.

Boris saw I was interested and said I had aptitude. I didn't know what that was when I was twelve, but if it meant he'd teach me things, I was happy.

We started looking for specific things to scavenge then: power packs, adaptors, splitters and cables and all that kind of stuff. In the end, we were able to help the whole gang. When we were on a major bit of scavenging around a wreck or a closed down worksite and we knew we would be there for a while, we would set up a perimeter with sensors and alarms. I would have to go back and dismantle it afterwards, but it would give us advance warning of the cops coming. Of course we only kept a little bit of what we fixed up. Most of it Boris would sell on and bring us back food with the money he made.

I could see Boris and the old man sizing each other up. Boris came right over and stood beside me and cleared his throat.

"What do you want?" he said.

"I've just offered Mouse a job," said the old man. "She's still deciding."

Boris looked down at me.

"What are you going to do, Mouse?" he asked.

I squinted up at him. It was the first time I'd thought of him as being an adult. Most of the time, he was just a big kid.

"What do you think I should do?"

Boris turned his gaze on the old man and for a moment, the two men looked at each other without speaking.

"Is it proper work?" he asked the man.

"We'll see," he said. "But I'll look after her."

Boris kept looking at the old man. I could hear him breathing. It was like I could hear him thinking.

"I think you should go," Boris said. "You'll know where to find us won't you?"

"Yeah," I said.

I gave a quick wave to the others as I went out with the old man. We walked out of the building onto the litter strewn access road. At the end of that, we reached the street proper. There were people on the sidewalks and cabs and private cars hummed by. In the distance, I could see the tall buildings of downtown with their lights just starting to come on.

We walked in silence. Then I saw a cop. The old man noticed me flinch.

"It's okay," he said gently. "You're with me. He won't trouble you."

We walked right past him, the cop giving the old man a deferential nod. He knew he was blueblood too. Cops aren't. Not the ones on the street anyway, although it doesn't stop them from acting all superior.

"How did you find us?" I asked.

He smiled. "I just went out and looked for vagrants. I knew the places where you hang out. I'm old and retired, you see, so I have time to watch."

"What's the job?"

"Are you brave?" he asked.

"Yes," I said. I was offended he had to ask.

"Well I'm afraid we've got rats in our roof. We need someone to set some traps in the roof spaces and the walls. There's not much room and you're just the right size to get in."

He chuckled.

"What?" I said suspiciously.

"I just had a funny thought. You're called Mouse, and I want you to catch some rats."

He chuckled again and I had to smile as well.

"Is that guy your Dad?" he asked.

"No," I said. Of course Boris wasn't my Dad. "I don't have a Dad."

"What about a Mom?" he said, his voice a little quieter this time.

"She died when I was ten," I said.

She died of the blood sickness. That was when I had to leave home. I went to live with my aunt after that. She had come and got me from my mother's house. I hardly knew her because she was vagrant and didn't get to see my mother very often. We lived in squats around the city. I missed my home at first, even though it had only been an apartment in the redblood districts. It had been comfortable and my things were there. But you can get used to anything, so I did get used to the wandering life we had, keeping out of the way of the cops. I got to be with the other vagrant kids. We seemed to be either running or hanging out. There was little reason to walk anywhere.

Then my aunt went and died too about a year later. Blood sickness too, of course. There was nobody else, so I just stayed with the other kids, forming our own gang. Sometimes there were adults around, like Boris, but we could look after ourselves. I didn't want any more family anyway. They just died. We knew the city well. That was my home, although none of it was mine.

We arrived at the old man's house. It was one of the bigger ones in a good part of town. I knew the area because the food pickings are always better in these parts.

A large redblood lady met us at the door. She had red cheeks and a headscarf covered her hair which strayed out from under the cloth in brown wisps. She eyed me with suspicion.

"What's this?" she asked the old man.

"Mrs Hunter, meet our rat catcher," said the old man with a smile.

I assumed she was their domestic. I could see why they hadn't asked her to do it. She was much too big to go into the roof.

"We should kit you out properly shouldn't we?" said the old man. "Could you fix her up with a head torch, some gloves and some poison please? I just have a call to make."

He smiled at me. "I'll come back soon and see how you've got on."

I was sorry to see him go, but I wasn't going to show it.

"Come with me," said Mrs Hunter and brought me into the kitchen. "Stand there and don't touch anything."

She went off to a side room and I scowled at her back. I wanted to touch everything. There were work benches and shining pots and pans and a giant refrigerator and a sink and big knives on the wall. I wanted a kitchen like that. I wanted to be able to cook in it, to be able to cook whatever I wanted.

She came back with a bag of rat bait and a headtorch.

"You look after that," he said. "I've only got the one."

"What about the gloves?" I said.

"I'm not wasting perfectly good gloves on you," she said. "Come with me."

I followed her, narrowing my eyes at her behind as she led the way up the stairs. I had decided that I didn't like Mrs Hunter.

I looked around me the whole time. I took in the carpets, the subtle tones of the walls, the paintings which hung on them, the light fittings. The doors were real wood. I wanted to run my fingers over them.

At the top of the stairs, three flights up, she opened a small hatch in the wall.

"In there," she said. "Spread the bait about."

I switched on the light and stepped into the dark.

I had to pull myself along using the joists. It was scary in the crawl-space. I was glad of the torch. It was on a strap around my head so I could keep my hands free.

For a few seconds, I thought it was going to be easy. Then I heard them. The rats were scurrying about in the darkness, alert to the knowledge that there was an intruder in their domain.

The space sure was narrow and it became narrower still whenever there was a joist. I had to shuffle along at an angle, worming my way through beams and roof supports.

I could feel my heart beating quickly, so I waited to calm down.

"Are you alright in there?" Mrs Hunter asked.

"Yes," I said. "I'm just getting used to the dark."

"Good, because I'm going to close the hatch. I don't want any of those rats in the house. Just push it open when you're done."

With that, the dim light from behind me vanished abruptly. I swept the headtorch around the space, up and down. There were grimy cobwebs and dust. I found a screw just lying there. It must have been left over from when they built the house. I put it in my pocket. As a vagrant kid, you're an instinctive scavenger.

The first rat I saw was just a dark shape moving out of the light. I didn't mind. I wasn't scared of rats: we saw them in the streets all the time and lots of those were big. It was just that I wasn't used to sharing a confined space with them.

Some of the rats in that space ran away when they heard me coming, but a few didn't. They stood their ground and twitched their tails at me. I looked at them and wondered if they knew why I was there and what I was going to do. I wondered if they were going to run at me and chew my eyes out.

I hissed at them and spat at them. If I did that now, Mrs Hunter would tell me it's not ladylike to spit, but I'd only just met Mrs Hunter then and anyway, she couldn't see me.

I had already laid a couple of baits, then as I was laying the next one, a big rat ran out of the darkness at me and tried to nip my hand. I stifled a shout of surprise that I didn't want anyone to think was a scream and shoved the bait trap in its face and pushed it away. It licked its whiskers after that. I thought it might die right there and then. I didn't realize rat poison doesn't work like that. I didn't know it was slow and horrible.

I wriggled about in there for an hour or two. It was the walls which were hardest because I had to climb down this narrow space, all the time thinking a rat was going to land on my head. I couldn't wait to get out of there, but I wasn't going to give up. I wanted to show Mrs Hunter I was better than her. I wanted to show them I could work hard and I didn't care how dirty I got. And I wasn't going to be scared off by a few rats.

When I finally clambered out of the access hatch, dirty and aching, the old man was there. He took my hand to help me out.

"Good work," he said and winked at me.

I smiled at him.

"Now, how about some pie? Mrs Hunter has made more than enough for the family."

I wasn't going to argue about that.

"Where can she sleep, Mrs Hunter?" he said.

"Sleep? She's not staying here is she?" said Mrs Hunter.

"Well we've got plenty of other things she'd be able to do that'll be a big help to you."

"Hasn't she got parents to go back to?"

"I look after myself," I said, looking at her with my arms crossed. I didn't want her thinking I needed people to look after me.

She gave me one of those I-wasn't-talking-to-you looks.

"But the Colonel – "

"Don't worry about the Colonel. I'll square it with him."

He turned to me.

"Better not tell anyone about the rats, Mouse. I think it's because we're so close to the hospital." He put on a sinister voice. "They feed on old body parts. Some say, they get fed deliberately." He winked at me again. "And there aren't supposed to be rats in a blueblood house are there? Certainly not ones that big."

I grinned. Now there are some blueblood men who might wink at you and it meant something quite unpleasant might happen to you if they could get hold of you. The old man's wink was quite different. It was like he was congratulating me on a job well done and saying he liked me at the same time.

Mrs Hunter rolled her eyes and bustled me out of the room. She showed me to a storeroom off the kitchen where I was allowed to sleep.

"Touch any food and you'll be out of here faster than your legs will carry you," she said to me. "But first, you need a shower. Make sure you scrub yourself hard. You're filthy."

It had been a very long time since I'd had a wash. We used to go in the ornamental ponds in some of the parks when we could get away with it, or in the fountains, but the cops would chase us out, so it was never much fun. This shower was pure luxury, despite Mrs Hunter shouting at me to hurry up from the corridor. It was hot, there was soap and no one was going to chase me away.

"Who's the Colonel?" I asked her.

"Colonel Hammond is a very important man. You mind how you behave if you meet him. He's been very good to me."

There were more jobs over the next few days. I was set to dusting every room and then I had to tidy up the garden. I had to work out what was weeds and what wasn't.

"I used to keep a kitchen garden," said Mrs Hunter, looking out at it. "But it all became a bit much for me."

That was a big job and it took me all week to start making inroads. Seeing how hard I worked, Mrs Hunter softened towards me, but I was still careful with her. As far as I was concerned, she'd made it very clear how she felt about me at the start.

I think it was Grandad Tennison who kept finding the jobs for me. That's how I came to think of the old man. He was the Colonel's father-in-law. He told me he was very pleased with my work, but I doubt the Colonel really was interested in what I had done. As far as he was concerned, I was just some lowly ranker in the household.

I met him on the same day I found out about Boris. One evening at the end of my first week at the Hammonds', I sneaked out into the city after I had finished all my jobs for the day and found the gang.

There were whoops when I walked in and Casey made a point of looking me up and down because I was wearing some old clothes that were new to him and too big for me. Then everyone became glum.

"What's up?" I asked.

"It's Boris," Casey said. My heart sank. "He was scavenging on his own. Pip saw the cops get him. They stuck him in a van and drove him away."

He would often get so focused on what he was doing that he didn't notice what was going on around him. I suppose that was how they got him. The best that would have happened would have been a labor camp. That's where they took all the vagrants they found.

I was feeling sad and empty when I returned to the Hammonds' house. I didn't notice the man at the front door until I almost walked into him. He shoved me back against the wall and stared at me hard.

"Where do you think you're going?"

I looked at his face knowing he must be Colonel Hammond. Where Mr Tennison's face was gentle, the Colonel's was hard with no spare flesh and his hair was cropped close. He looked like everything I had learned to fear about the Trooper Corps.

"Please sir, I said, Mr Tennison hired me. I've been helping Mrs Hunter."

He stared at me a little longer, then released me.

"Oh. You're her," he said. "So go on inside and help then."

Then he turned and went inside himself. I stood out there a little longer, wondering if I should still go in. Something about him frightened me. Then I saw a rat. It was crawling across the yard in front of the house, dribbling blood out of its mouth. I felt sick.

What cemented me in the household was when Mrs Hunter became ill. She was confined to her bed and I had to take over all the jobs in the house. I had been watching her in the kitchen and doing things to help, like chopping things up and stirring.

One afternoon, I was bringing some soup to her. I had heard the doctor arrive. When I went in, I stopped in my tracks because the Colonel was there as well. The doctor was handing him a tab, the screen flashed at me as it reflected the light of the window for a moment.

"Just scan your creds please, Colonel," he said.

Colonel Hammond did as he was asked, using the tab to do so, then handed it back.

Mrs Hunter was looking puzzled.

The doctor bent down to his case and pulled out a small flask of a clear liquid with a slight blue tinge to it. I thought it was water, but it was a little thicker.

"You must drink all this down," said the doctor.

"What is it, sir?" Mrs Hunter asked.

"It's a nanomed solution. It will be effective all night and perhaps part of tomorrow if you stay in bed."

Her eyes opened wide with wonder and she turned to the Colonel. "You're doing this for me? I'm so grateful."

Colonel Hammond nodded brusquely.

"We need you back on duty, Mrs Hunter."

I put the tray down and stomped out of the room. I was angry. I was so angry I could feel tears coming so I forced them back. I went into the garden and jabbed a fork into the ground, vaguely aiming at some weeds. Then I sat back on my haunches. My mother had never had the Hammonds to give her nanomeds. She wouldn't have died. And neither would my aunt. I hated Mrs Hunter even more after that. Not to her face; I was too smart for that. I needed to keep on the right side of her if I was to stay in the house. But I hated her because she had lived here for years, she had a home and she had nanomeds when she needed them. And she wasn't even a blueblood.

That was when I decided it. I was going to stay in this house as long as I could. After all, it was much safer than being vagrant on the street.

[1]

MRS HUNTER HANDS ME A tray of tea and biscuits.

"Take this up to Mr Tennison," she says. "Tell him the Colonel would like him to be at dinner. Mr Willard's coming."

I take the tray up the three flights of stairs to the bedroom at the top. He is sitting at his desk when I open the door.

"Hello Grandad."

He smiles and puts down a book he's been reading, setting it on the desk.

"No one else upstairs then?" he says.

"How do you know?"

"You wouldn't call me Grandad if they were."

That's because the family would be outraged to hear me being so familiar with him, even after the six years I've been here. They caught me saying it once and put me on short rations for a week. That only taught me to be more careful.

I put the tray on the small table in the middle of the room.

"Are you going to eat downstairs this evening?"

He grunts.

"View's better from up here," he says, gesturing vaguely at the window. "It's a lovely sky tonight." He looks at me. "And none of them call me Grandad anymore," he adds.

"Don't they?"

"Those boys reckon they're too old for it. And to make it worse, Lee started calling me 'sir' when he got into his military training."

He starts coughing. I go to help him, but he holds up his hand to me as he gains control of the spasm.

"I'm alright, Mouse."

"You're not. You should take the medicine."

"It's not medicine they're offering. I've got enough of those robots inside me."

"They're too small to be robots."

"What are they then?"

"Well, they're just...machines, I guess. They're supposed to help you."

"You guess."

"You wouldn't mind if they linked you up to a machine in the hospital."

"I wouldn't, but you come off those. Once they put those nanomeds in you, they're in there for life, stitching you up on the inside, mucking about with you."

"I thought they could flush them out," I say.

"In theory, but what blood would they put in its place? They're not going to want some redblood's dirty blood are they, no offence? And they want to keep the robots anyway. It's not normal I tell you. I've got white blood cells and platelets which are perfectly good at that sort of thing and all quite natural."

"So you always say," I smile at him. He's off again. Sometimes I do it just to get him going. "But why did you get them in the first place?"

"Everyone with money or the right connections was getting them. And who wouldn't? When most of the world has been reduced to rubble and the air's rank with the biotoxins our glorious leaders threw at each other, everyone would have taken them if they could. I'll say this for them, they're little miracles. I can understand a Mars rocket, but I'm damned if I understand nanomeds. Still, that doesn't mean I ever liked them. Nanomeds are like taking medicine when you're not sick. You cope without them don't you?"

"I haven't got any choice. They only give them to their favorite redbloods. And even then it's just a drink for short term effect. You can't have redbloods becoming bluebloods because we don't know how to behave in polite society."

"Well I think you're better off without them, even if it means you die early."

"You'd rather be a redblood?" I say.

"I'd rather not have nanomeds running around inside my body, but these days as you know too well, they do a lot more for you than just being better for your health."

"But you do have them and all the other benefits that go with it. I'll never be as strong as I could be if I had them."

He shakes his head.

"No, you're stronger for being without them," he says. "What you do is all down to you."

He's about to go on when he starts coughing again. When he has recovered, he goes on. "We didn't need them on the Mars missions and health was critical there. But that was before the war."

"Wouldn't it have helped them on Mars though? I thought it was pretty tough setting up on a new planet."

"People have been exploring new lands for centuries, Mousey. Mars is no different, except you can't breathe and it's a lot colder." He grins. "I'm proud to say, they're doing very well, last we heard. Last of the pioneers. All settled now."

He gets that faraway look in his eyes. Grandad is ex-Airforce, but he worked on the Mars program. I like hearing him talk about it. It's funny to think that even now there are tens of thousands of people living way out there who were untouched by the war. All it meant was that the program stopped and no one else went out to join them. They're on their own now.

I always make a point of looking after Grandad. He's old and ill now and I know he's not going to be around forever. I try not to think about what might happen to me if he dies. It was Grandad who brought me the bracelet creds that said I worked for the Hammonds, but I won't be able to do this job for much longer. Once the boys are in the Corps full time, they won't need Mrs Hunter and me at home. I need to start finding myself something else to keep me off the streets. I need to look after myself because no one else is going to.

Grandad has told me that he likes having me around. He said I was a breath of fresh air in the Hammond household what with Sherman and Lee growing up as army brats. You only have to look at their names. Naming them after Civil War generals must have been the work of their father. They were pretty much born for military service. I think it was because Grandad worked on the Mars program that he was different from the rest of the family and from the other military types who came around. They had a different mindset.

"We were about exploring, not killing," he said to me once.

He had made it his job to know who each of his team was and what they did. He would tell me about it and he would include details about the people in his team, who they were and what their jobs involved.

So when he gets that look in his eyes, I know what he's thinking. He was due for the next flight if the war hadn't happened. He'd worked on the Mars project for years; watched thousands of settlers head out before him and finally it was his chance to go. But with the war, all Mars flights were cancelled. He flew military aircraft instead. He shakes his head again, remembering.

"For nearly a century we were a hopeful race, heading out to the stars. You can't understand what it was like. Not like now. All it takes is a few idiots to change the world for the worse. It's funny how changing things for the better is so much harder."

It all happened years before I was born. I've only known things as they are now. The rest is as distant to me as a fairy story, and I've heard few enough of those.

I look up at Mars sometimes. Grandad's told me where to find it. It's just another star, flickering red if you stare at it long enough.

"Isn't it time you joined the regiment for dinner?" I ask.

He chuckles. That's what he calls the family.

"The Colonel's home tonight. That big do at headquarters was cancelled."

"And how would you know that?"

"Sherman told me."

Sherman's the younger son. I know what's coming now.

"Sherman eh?" He looks at me with a twinkle in his eye. "You watch that lad, Mousey. For a start, his blood is too rich for you and he's an eye for the girls."

"I can look after myself."

"That's what I'm afraid of."

"Mrs Hunter told me to tell you that Mr Willard is coming for dinner and the Colonel would like you to come down."

He rolls his eyes.

"Who is this Willard?" I ask.

"Oh some businessman. He owns various big companies. Just some ego with a lot of money. Clearly my son-in-law wants to show off the old war hero."

"So are you joining them or not? You can't be up here all the time."

"I'm not here all the time. I go out for plenty of walks."

"You know what I mean."

"Oh alright, I'll come down, but just to shut you up."

He mutters something about making himself decent and I go back down ahead of him with the tray.

On my way to the kitchen, Lee suddenly comes around a corner and almost bumps into me. He's head and shoulders taller than me and his shoulders are probably twice as wide, so I'm glad he manages to stop himself from colliding with me.

He's the older of the Colonel's sons. He's twenty and has been in the Corps for a year. I have to admit, the uniform looks good on him, but then most things do. His dark hair is cropped short and shows off the clean lines of his face. His eyes are dark and I'd say they showed hidden depths if he wasn't such a prick.

When I first came to the house, he played with me sometimes, but then he started to keep away from me, treat me like I was a piece of dirt. That's how it's been ever since. He can barely stomach being in the same room as me.

He is struggling with the idea of me now. He recoils, not so much from not wanting to bump into me, but in case he actually touches me. I swear he winces.

"Sorry," I say, because of course I know it's going to be my fault.

He looks away, not even wanting to meet my eyes and mutters something.

"Sorry?" I say again, but this time I'm just stirring, making him talk to me.

He clears his throat.

"I said watch where you're going, Muswell."

Muswell. Even the Colonel calls me Mouse, but not him. Can't go being familiar with a redblood.

He goes past me without another word. Frankly, I was lucky to get that, even if he was the one rushing around blind corners.

There comes a thundering down the stairs. I know who that is without turning around. An arm claps around my shoulder just to prove it. Sherman.

The brothers couldn't be any more different if they tried. I could list three things in common: their father, the fact that they've been bred for the military since they could walk. The third thing is that they're both good looking, but whereas Lee is brooding, Sherman is cheerful and blue-eyed with blond hair that always strays beyond regulation length and then takes on a mind of its own. After Grandad, he's the closest thing to a ray of sunshine in this tight-assed household.

"Hey Mouse," he says with an eyebrow raised with mock sternness. "You better be more careful. You almost knocked my big brother flying. You might ruin his beautifully pressed uniform."

Sherman's wearing a similar dark green uniform to his brother, but it still has the yellow cadet flashes on the collar. He's nineteen now and will be passing out soon. They've been training for this all their lives, so I know both of them are streets ahead of most recruits who start in the Trooper Corps.

He ruffles my hair and walks on. That always irritates me and he knows it; which is why he does it, so I refuse to give him the satisfaction of complaining. I pull it away from my collar.

I've just come out of the kitchen having left the tray when Grandad plods heavily down the stairs. Mrs Hunter emerges from the dining room where she's been laying out dinner. She scolds Grandad for avoiding them, like that'll encourage him to join them again. For a housekeeper, she's pretty relaxed around the family, but like I said, she's been around since before the boys were born and has been the only one providing anything like affection to them as they were growing up.

For a moment, I watch through the door. Sherman punches his grandfather on the arm and Lee salutes. He salutes! It's a bad enough way to greet his own father. I don't understand why he cannot see his grandfather doesn't appreciate it.

The last one in is the Colonel. It would never do to be early and he would never be late either. I swear he checked his watch before walking in. He's ramrod straight.

"Good evening, General," he says when he sees his father-in-law.

I sometimes forget Grandad was a one star general. Maybe he's just from another time when the world was more innocent. I wish they'd lighten up.

Since the war, there have been few people left to fight. From what I hear on the live-stream and from overheard conversations, the other countries in the world are sick, dying or dead already. The Corps defends us from Rads, pirates and raiders, but with the coasts contaminated, that's a natural barrier anyway, and the live-stream always says the Rads are nothing to worry about.

Living in a military family though, I see it quite differently. I know the real threat is the Rads. Why is the Corps so strong if there's really only a few unthreatening Rads hiding out in the wilderness and in the underbellies of the cities?

Sherman talks to me about it sometimes. He says the Rads are becoming stronger and stronger and the Corps needs to stamp down harder on them. He says they have stolen military grade equipment and that he has heard that redblood troopers have begun to desert and join the Rads. There have been explosions in some of the cities, even Corps bases have been attacked. The live-stream tells us the Rads want to overthrow society, that they're anarchists, that they will do anything to damage the state.

They certainly don't help the rest of us redbloods. We are treated badly enough already, but it doesn't take much for any of the rest of us to be treated as terrorists and anti-social elements. I have heard of people being taken away for saying something that was considered seditious or looking at a blueblood in the wrong way. They have become more suspicious of us and treat us worse. There's nothing we can do about it. I've seen redbloods shoved around in the street and there are places where we are simply not allowed to go so that we don't lower the tone for the bluebloods or expose them to disease.

Maybe there is a good reason for that. We redbloods do not live as long as the bluebloods do. We're more likely to become ill and we die younger like my mother did. A forty or a fifty year old redblood is considered old. Bluebloods can live twice as long and more, but then they have the nanomeds to help them out.

Grandad looks up and sees me in the hallway and winks, then Mrs Hunter shuts the door. I stare at its polished wood for a moment, then go and see what leftovers I can find in the kitchen.

Occasionally they actually feed me, but Mrs Hunter knows I scavenge my own food and after more than six years, she trusts me not to take anything I shouldn't. I'm also not a bad cook now and I like to experiment. Mrs Hunter even lets me cook sometimes, but she doesn't tell the Hammonds when I do it. I think she's afraid they'll think my cooking is so good, they won't need her any more. It would certainly help my position if she wasn't around, but that would be cruel.

Unlike Mrs Hunter, I don't have a job title. I'm just Mouse. 'Mouse, get this; Mouse do that.' But I'm almost eighteen now and beginning to feel too old to be scurrying about doing all the things that Mrs Hunter doesn't like to do herself or feels are beneath her.

The trouble is, they own me, not like a slave – although it feels like that – no, I'm free to go anytime I want. It's just that I'd have nowhere to go, nowhere to live and nothing to eat. I would become vagrant again, at risk of being rounded up and given unpleasant things to do in the worst parts of the city. I had enough of that when I was a kid. I need this place until I have something else and if I play my cards right, maybe they'd give me draughts of nanomeds if I became sick, just like they do for Mrs Hunter. So, despite all the boredom and drudgery of the Hammond household, I know I've got it cushy compared to a hopeless life working out of a compound until I died of overwork, starvation or the cold.

[2]

MRS HUNTER SENDS ME OUT to the market. She might not let on to anyone else that I can cook, but she's happy to trust me with shopping for fresh produce. That was a chore she gave up as soon as she felt she could trust me with it. She didn't like the crowds, the smells, the bargaining. In short, she didn't like all the things I did like.

You've got to have an eye for the right stuff when you go to the market. It's where you can get the best things and the worst things too. This means it's a meeting place for everyone.

I enjoy getting out of the house. I might not miss living on the streets, but I still enjoy being on them. They're full of life and I admit, I miss the excitement now. It was often exhausting being on the alert all the time, but at least I felt alive. At the Hammonds, I'm safe, but bored. That's why I stick my nose into anything new I find.

You can tell redbloods from bluebloods on the street. They're often smaller or paler and more sickly, but it's also obvious from the job they do. They're poorer of course and they're also the ones doing the work.

There is a big refuse truck moving slowly down the street with men and women collecting garbage from outside apartment blocks. Others follow behind cleaning the street. I glance through shop windows. Shop staff are redbloods, but managers are usually bluebloods. In front of me, someone jumps out of the front of a car and opens the door for a blueblood seated in the back.

A cop is strolling down the other side of the road. Most cops are redbloods and I can tell this one's redblood just from the expression on his face. He's looking all superior, as if the uniform can make him a blueblood. There are redbloods in the Corps too. It's the easiest way off the street, the easiest job to find. Some of the poorest go there. They prefer it to the labor camps, even with the risk of getting yourself killed. Most of them don't see it like that though. They believe the live-stream. For them, the military is a cushy job where they get fed, housed and clothed.

I often run to the market and then walk back with the shopping, I enjoy the exercise. There are several markets around the city and I assume they're all the same. This one is in a huge hall and it is always busy.

There are all bands of society in here. There's bluebloods at one end and the redbloods at the other end. But in the middle are better off redbloods who mostly eat the packaged food that's processed out on the farms on the plains. I've never been there, but Sherman says I wouldn't want to. He says there's nothing to see but flat fields as far as the eye can see.

The poorest redbloods, which is most of them, can't afford the packaged food and prepare what they can from what they can afford. They buy it here at the market or go to slop houses where someone else has cooked the same things, but not told you exactly what else has gone in it.

One side of the market is taken up with huge bulk stores of flour, fruit and vegetables. I know it well because it's what I had to eat when I was on the street. I take pleasure in walking right on past them as I enter. I come in this way to remind myself, to make sure I appreciate where I live now. This is the old, the rotten and the deformed produce. There always seems to be a surprising amount of it. This is all the food that is not good enough to go in the packaged food and which is certainly not good enough to go into the part of the market where I am heading.

I make my way over to the far side of the hall. There is a door there. It is guarded and I have to show my bracelet to them to show I am with a family. There was a riot a few years ago. Before I was born. It was put down very brutally. Boris told me they left the blood stains on the floor for weeks afterwards as a kind of warning.

In this part of the market is the best produce. The atmosphere changes as soon as you cross the threshold. There's a smell of green and freshness, baked bread, ground coffee, the sharp scent of ripe fruit. Fish gleams silver, the meat is red and inviting.

Other families have a shopper and have the food delivered. We do the shopping ourselves. Mrs Hunter and I pride ourselves in our taste and choice. We refuse to trust anyone else to do it for us. I can smell and feel and squeeze, although the stallholders don't let me do that as much as they do the bluebloods.

When I come to the cheese counter, I select my cheese by the vendor. One is a nasty man who doesn't seem to care about my bracelet. He's actually told me he doesn't want my dirty blood near his cheese. This means he's lost my business. Sherman came with me once, but I steered him away from that stall. Of course I made sure the vendor saw Sherman was blueblood and then that he saw me deliberately steer him away.

When I finish shopping, the backpack I'm carrying is heavy. I feel like a hunter, unlike Mrs Hunter who, ironically, is probably sitting on her large backside watching the live-stream.

Getting back to the house, I drop the food off in the kitchen and sneak away before Mrs Hunter can give me any more jobs to do. As I do, I hear a shout of frustration from the family room. I peer around the door and see Sherman at the main console shaking his head at the settings. He sees me before I can pull my head back.

"Get in here, Mouse!" he says.

I walk in.

"Sounds like you're having a few problems."

"Live-stream has gone offline and I can't get it on my tab either."

"That sounds odd. Are you sure it's not just you?"

He narrows his eyes at me.

"What are you saying? Are you saying that I broke it?"

"Not at all, but you may have inadvertently changed one of your settings."

He frowns and gives me a playful punch on the arm.

"Well why don't you apply your pretty brain to fixing it for me," he says.

I give him a superior look and elbow him out of the way. Sometimes I am surprised at what I can get away with around Sherman. One day I think I might go too far, but he usually treats me as if I was actually one of the family, albeit, one he can order around.

I delve into the settings, then dig into some diagnostics.

"What the hell are those?" he asks.

"Looks like it wasn't you. Well done," I smirk.

He punches me again. A little harder this time, but I pretend not to notice.

"I need to check the main router," I say. "Could you let me into it?"

In most houses, the main router would be an open part of the house, but this is a military household and the Colonel has an extra layer of hardware security as well as the usual software encryption.

It's funny how I got to be the family tech. Technology is the other thing I pride myself at. Boris started me off and I've taught myself so much since then. I watch any techs who come over to do any installs or mods and grill them with questions. I dig around on the stream too and the rest is just me playing around, making mistakes and seeing where they get me. As the Hammonds' domestic, the scope of my duties expands to anything I can do. I learn fast and I like to branch out into things more interesting than poking around in roof spaces.

I follow Sherman to the Colonel's study. He's not in there, so Sherman unlocks the cabinet.

"Something's different," I say.

"Probably. There was a Corps tech here while you were out."

I roll my eyes and have a look. I could see from the diagnostics that there was a dead line, so now I just have to find the reason for it.

"Do you have a flashlight?" I ask.

Sherman hands me his stylus which has a light in the end. I use it to peer around. There's a big chunk of military gear in here. It is sealed inside a box that looks like it would survive a bomb blast. There's some new patching which I guess was what today's tech was handling. It doesn't look right.

"That tech who came today, did he look like he knew what he was doing?"

"I don't know. I just checked his creds and let him in."

"Young guy?"

"Yeah. What's up?"

"I think he's cross-swapped the feeder lines."

Sherman cocks his head at me.

"That sounds painful," he says.

"Well it would kill the live-stream and probably disrupt any other civilian feed into the house. Have you tried the net feed on your tab or are you tied into this?"

"I don't know, I just use the damn thing," he says. "Can you fix it?"

"Not without cracking the Corps gear you've got here and I'd need a tank to get into it."

"Perhaps I could arrange one."

"Or maybe you could just get the tech back in to fix it."

"I'll see what I can do. What do I tell him?"

"Like I said, he's cross-swapped the feeder lines. Corps comms will still work fine, but he's canned your civ stuff."

"Okay," he says. "You're not stiffing me are you, because you'll pay if you do."

"Of course not. Look, I'd speak to him myself, but Corps techs don't like to be told what to do by a civ redblood."

"True."

"You can tell him he owes you one. It's a fool mistake."

"Sweet. I get owed a favor from an incompetent tech."

"Well hopefully this is one mistake he won't make twice."

"You should join the tech corps when we finally kick you out."

I leave him to it. The tech made a basic mistake, easy to make, but it shows he didn't test it properly. If the Colonel had been around, his goose would have been cooked. I feel good about having found the problem, but that last comment has got me thinking once again about how precarious life is here.

[3]

I MAKE IT MY BUSINESS to know what's going on in the house. It makes me feel like I've got a stake in things, but it's also about survival. I'll loiter in rooms being busy while conversations are going on and you'd be amazed how clearly I can hear through doors.

Mrs Hunter hears things too and she couldn't keep a secret if her life depended on it. She may be stern, but she also needs to talk and if she knows something, she just has to tell someone.

My other main source of information is Sherman. I know he's jealous of Lee even though he mocks him. He's jealous of his ability to focus and work hard. He wants to pass his cadetship as a lieutenant, not an ensign. I tell him it's not going to happen. I tell Sherman he needs to work harder, he needs to stop going out until late with his buddies, he needs to lose his sense of humor and avoid talking to redbloods.

Then he'll chuck me under the chin and say "I was all set to take your advice until that last one."

I know he's a flirt. He's got blueblood girls hanging around him, but I've known him for years and I see their faces if he flirts with me in front of them. He does it to get a reaction out of them. They don't say anything because they can't, but he doesn't notice their eyes like another girl does. That gives me a little bit of pleasure though, because, pet mouse as I am, they actually seem to see me as a threat.

After so many years of sniffing out what's happening around the house, this morning I can sense that something is going on. There's been a tension ever since that family meal. The Colonel flew out the next morning and he's been gone a week now. All I've managed to find out is that something is going on up north, but since then, there's been a sense of waiting for something to happen. In the end, I ask Grandad.

"It's just Lee waiting for his first combat posting," he says. "His father's had him kicking his heels in a staff role."

"Why?" I ask. "Is he protecting him?"

"No. He's giving Lee a well-rounded military education. While Lee can't wait for a bit of action, it's good for him to see the machine that drives the military, to understand that it takes two soldiers to support every soldier in the field, making sure they're supplied with food and ammunition and all the other things that makes the front line bearable."

"The front line?" I scoff. "You make it sound like a war."

"Don't believe everything you see on the stream," he says. Then he turns back to his tab and I know I won't get anything else out of him.

It takes another week for something to happen. It's the evening and I'm fixing cabling in the comms trunking. It's in a unit under the stairs. I know it's happened because Lee appears from his room in a state of uncharacteristic excitement.

"Sherm! It's come!"

Then he sees me and his eyes slide off me like I'm a pile of sick and he looks just as uncomfortable. I hear Sherman come out behind me.

"Show me!" he calls. There's excitement and envy in his voice. Lee passes him his tab.

"You're going north too!" Sherman says. "The Colonel's posting you with him!"

"He said I would learn something up there," Lee says. "He said I'd get some action."

Sherman rolls his eyes to the ceiling.

"Man, I can't wait til I pass out."

"It's only six months," says Lee.

"Might as well be six years," he says.

Two days later, Sherman finds me in the garden. I've pretty much taken it over from Mrs Hunter. I like to grow my own herbs and vegetables because then I know what's going into growing them. Grandad arranged to have some good soil delivered.

"Have you ever been out of the city?" he asks.

"Barely," I say.

"I'm going north," he says.

"What, north with your brother?"

"Yes." His eyes are gleaming.

"How did you manage that? You're just a cadet."

"A bit less of the 'just a cadet please', Miss Mouse. I've managed to wangle myself a tactical placement."

"Very nice," I say, none the wiser. "What's that?"

"Cadets need to do placements around operational units as part of training, to observe, be useful. You know, learn a thing or two without being actually on active duty."

"And you got one with Lee? How did you manage that?"

He winks.

"Charm."

I can believe that.

"And calling in a few favors," he adds.

I can believe that too.

"So pack your bag," he says.

I frown, puzzled.

"You want me to pack your bag?"

"No, I can do that. I want you to pack yours."

"Why?"

I'm suddenly confused. A hundred thoughts are flying around my head, but it's obvious really. Now that everyone is out of the house, they won't need me anymore. Mrs Hunter will be more than enough to keep the ship afloat. They've no further use for me. I feel panic and resentment at the same time. What am I going to do? And why am I tied to this family? What will I do when I'm no longer living here? The least they can do is find me a new position somewhere. It's almost impossible to find something from a state of vagrancy. It's illegal to be a vagrant, yet if you're not employed, you're immediately classed as a vagrant.

"Have you found me another position?" I say. I know I'm stammering. I can't help myself.

He winks again.

"I have."

I'm relieved, but this is still the unknown, this is still not me controlling what's happening and it's at times like this that it really comes home to me. I *am* a slave.

"You're coming north with me," he says.

"What?"

For a moment, I'm not thinking anything.

"Because I'm not actually an officer yet, I don't get an attendant provided by the Corps, but I'm quite entitled to bring my own. So, I thought you might like an outing. We're flying up with Lee."

"Who knows about this?"

I'm playing for time really. I don't know what to think about this yet. I don't know if it's a good thing or a bad thing.

"You and me."

"Lee won't like it."

Sherman shrugs. "He doesn't have to."

"When are we leaving?"

"Tomorrow. So you'd better go pack. And I've left some clothes on your bed. You'll need to be a bit smarter up there. You know, look the part."

I narrow my eyes at him and stalk off, but he's right about my clothes. They're all past their best. I've never had any new ones and I tend to end up with utilitarian ones which are a size or more too big for me. So when I get to my room, I'm amazed.

Lying on the bed are two sets of clothes. They look brand new. They're not actually uniforms, but they look like them. They're green, but not the smart dark green of the service uniforms I see Sherman, Lee and their father wearing normally. One is olive green and the other is a little paler. I hold them up.

There's a double-breasted jacket which is shaped at the waist, cream cotton shirts to go underneath and matching trousers which are tight on the hips and shaped to the ankle. He's even provided boots. All of it has a military air, but it smacks of style as well. What isn't military is the underwear. That I might not put on because I know Sherman is just going to imagine I'm wearing it. I think I'll stick to my own.

I hold the uniform up to myself in the mirror, then I put it down, tie my hair back and look again. I look smart, but my eyes stare back at me quizzically.

What should I do? No one seems to have said that I have to go or that anything will happen to me if I don't. Yet this is a chance to get out of this house, get out of this city, to see something else, to ride in an aircraft. It feels like an opportunity, like something I shouldn't pass up. There didn't seem to be any doubt in Sherman's mind that I'd be going. He even went to the trouble of buying me some clothes. Should I be flattered? No, he was only buying them so I wouldn't let him down.

Once more I feel resentful. I resent his presumption that I'd be going. I don't think it even occurs to him that I might not go. Part of me wants to refuse for that very reason, but even as I think that, I know that I'd be disappointed if I didn't go. I want to go. It's as simple as that.

I go to find Grandad and tell him.

He puts his tab down, folds his fingers together and looks at me without saying anything for a moment.

"What?" I ask.

"Take care of yourself up there."

"I will. I've been doing it since I was little."

"Bases full of soldiers are quite a different thing. Keep a low profile and don't rely on Sherman to look after you."

I laugh. "Don't worry. I've known him a long time."

"And remember it is a war zone up there."

"Really?"

"Remember I told you not to believe everything you see on the live-stream? Well the reason there's a base up there is because they're trying to locate Rad training camps. They've got them hidden out in the wilderness."

"But I'll be safe in the camp," I say, a little uncertainly.

"So stay in the camp." He winks. "See you in a month."

I wake early the next morning and cannot get back to sleep. I'm excited and nervous. I've dressed in the olive green outfit and when Sherman appears, he looks me up and down and smiles smugly out of one side of his mouth.

"Fits you well. I've got such a good eye."

I don't know whether to hug him or punch him.

We ride to the airfield in silence, each of us full of our own thoughts. We show our creds to the sentries on the gate. My heart is in my mouth as they scan them as I think they're going to turn me away, but then they're passing them back to us.

Sherman catches my eye as we drive through and smirks. We're stopped at a second checkpoint and we have to leave the cab at this point. Civilian vehicles aren't allowed any further. I feel kind of special.

We hoist our bags over our shoulders and walk past a number of two story buildings. Then at the end, we come to an open area and a big green copter is squatting on the ground in front of us. Personnel are loading up pallets of boxes and I can see Lee watching them. There is an officer with a tab checking off the consignment. Sherman shows him our creds and he waves us through.

We walk over to the copter. Well, I walk; Sherman is swaggering. Lee turns as we reach the aircraft and I immediately realize Sherman hasn't told him anything yet. He looks at both of us, then turns to Sherman angrily.

"What's going on here?"

"Tactical placement, big brother."

"Really? Show me your directive."

Sherman hands him his tab then watches him reading it, a sly grin on his face. Lee hands it back, but his face has lost none of its anger.

"What about her?"

He neither points at me, nor looks at me. I might as well not be there.

"Mouse? She's going as my attendant. Like it says at the bottom, cadets are to be treated as junior officers and can provide their own attendant if they are able. We're able."

Lee seems lost for words.

"We're going to a war zone," he manages.

"She won't be outside the base. It'll all be fine. What can happen?"

Lee seems to be weighing this up, pressing his lips together. He shifts his weight from one foot to the other.

"Does father know?" he asks.

"He's probably seen the placement lists for himself."

"I mean about her."

Sherman shrugs.

"He's not going to care one way or the other, is he?"

Lee looks at the cargo being loaded for a moment.

"No," he says through gritted teeth. "No, he wouldn't."

And for once I agree with Lee. He wouldn't care what happened to me. He barely notices me now. Up there, I could probably walk right past him and he wouldn't even notice it was me.

"All right," says Lee. "Let's go."

[4]

AS IT TURNS OUT, THERE are only the three of us and the pilots. The rest of the copter is taken up with supplies. We strap ourselves in at the front of the cargo bay. One of the pilots comes through to check on us.

"We're all good back here," says Sherman grinning. Lee just gives him a professional nod, trying to distance himself from us.

The engine starts up, sending a throbbing through the whole aircraft. Suddenly it lurches into the air. My stomach leaps and I look at Lee and Sherman, but they look quite relaxed, so this must be normal. I hope they didn't notice me jump. I don't want either of them to think I'm nervous.

I twist around in my seat and watch the ground drop away below us. Soon, the buildings are small and I can see the whole city. The river loops through the center of town. There is the dock area of Waterside, an area I know well for its rich pickings and maze of streets and buildings large enough to hide in. I can see the smarter districts where the Hammonds live and the much larger spawl of the redblood areas. Then the view opens wider and I can see plains disappearing into the murky distance. Out there are towns and the farms that supply K-City and the other inland cities which survived the war. I've never seen them except on the live stream. This is my first view of a wider world.

For a few minutes I get to gaze on all this, then we're bumping through clouds and I can't see anything anymore.

I don't understand why the clouds are making us bump, but I check on the brothers again and judge from their reaction that this is still normal. Sherman's watching me. He grins.

"Cool eh?" he shouts above the drone of the engine.

I nod and turn back to the window and the cloud rushing by outside. We're soon above it and the ride smooths out. I can still see snatches of the land through the cloud, but the sun is shining on us uninterrupted.

I sit and wait for something else to happen, but it doesn't. Lee and Sherman both go to sleep and one of the pilots comes back and pulls a couple of flasks out of a carry case just behind the cockpit. He pours a couple of coffees and is about to take them back with him when he sees me watching him. He holds one out to me and I smile and take it. He nods, pours another one for himself and disappears into the cockpit.

I like the gesture. It makes me feel as though I'm supposed to be here. Even though I'd been through all those checkpoints, I still felt as though I was an imposter and someone was about to come out and send me home, or worse, back to the streets. But no one's asking questions anymore and I feel that here, above the clouds, I've escaped. In transit at least, I'm nobody, not a redblood, just a speck in the sky.

When I finish the drink I put the cup on the ground between my feet. The boys are still asleep and there's nothing to do. I didn't get a good sleep last night, so I follow their lead.

When I wake up, I'm refreshed. Lee and Sherman are both awake too. Lee is reading on his tab. Sherman is standing, leaning into the cockpit chatting to the pilots.

I unbuckle myself, stand up and stretch. Lee looks up briefly and then away, as if he'd forgotten it was me. I take a walk around the cabin circling the cargo, then go up to the front and peer over Sherman's shoulder. The view is way better from the cockpit. The blue sky smiles above and white clouds pass by below us. The pilots turn to see who the newcomer is.

"My attendant," says Sherman and I know he's grinned at the pilots because they grin too before looking back to the controls.

Sherman points into the distance where the cloud is thicker and higher.

"That's where we're going. You see that longer line of higher cloud? The mountains are on the other side of that."

"The mountains?" I ask. I'm nervous now. "We're not going over them are we?"

"No," says Sherman, smiling. "Still too much toxicity and radiation over that side. The Borealis Base is close to the mountains though."

During the war, the land west of the mountains was hit hardest by the nukes. No one lives over there and no one goes over there. They say there's nothing to see anyway unless you're into ruins and mutated wildlife.

The distant clouds come closer and closer.

"Better get back and strap in," says the pilot who gave me coffee. "The turbulence will bounce us around a bit more once we get into those, but once we do, you know we're not that far from the base."

We do as we're told and within a few minutes the copter's bumping around again. I get used to it and relax into my seat and feel like I'm becoming a bit of a pro at this. The turbulence becomes heavier and we are rocking harder now. There's a change in the engine noise and I feel lighter.

"We're descending," says Sherman. He looks at his watch. "A bit early for the final approach unless we've made good time. Maybe they're just getting beneath the weather."

We continue to descend and the movement decreases.

"Yup, look, there's the ground," says Sherman. "Can't see the base though."

I've just closed my eyes when there's a bigger jolt than any of the others. I open them again.

"That was a flash, did you see it?" says Lee. He's looking alert now.

"Lightning," says Sherman.

But the engine noise has just increased too.

"What's going on?" I ask.

"I'll see," says Sherman, but Lee has already unbuckled and moved to the cockpit door. He opens it and leans in.

I turn to look out of the window again. There are grey clouds above us now, but below I can see forest, trees as far as the eye can see. I'm mesmerized. I've never seen that many trees before.

"We're under fire!"

It's Lee. He's shouting from the cockpit door. Even Sherman looks startled this time.

There's another big jolt and a much louder bang. Suddenly it's windy. Lee staggers back out of the cockpit and my eyes widen in horror. There's blood and worse over the front of his uniform. For a moment I think it's his, then I realize it must be the pilots'. Just as I do, the copter begins to buck wildly.

Something unspoken goes between the brothers and Sherman is unbuckling and groping forwards.

"What's happening?" I manage.

Lee looks at me and for a moment I think he's coming over, then he frowns and looks away.

"Ground fire. I'll try to fly it."

Lee has done some copter training, so I just hope he's been doing enough. Sherman follows him into the cockpit. Terror starts to build in my stomach. Something has happened to the pilots. I'm cold too. With the cockpit glass smashed, the wind's knifing down into the cabin. A few loose bits of paper are whipping about in the wind.

Then the copter starts to spin. We're losing height quickly: my stomach is dropping. I tighten my harness over my chest and grip the seat with both hands. The engine pitch has risen. Sherman reappears, lurching against the movement of the aircraft. He's dragging one of the pilots and dumps him roughly just inside the cabin. The man is still wearing his flying helmet, but there's a ragged red mess where his neck and upper chest should be. I feel bile rising and look away, but the whirling of the copter isn't helping me. I screw my eyes shut and force away the feeling.

Suddenly the spinning stops, but we're still whirling from side to side and it also still feels like we're losing height.

I hear Lee shouting.

"Go back!"

Sherman comes in again, staggering against the movement of the copter and grabbing hold of seats and hand rails above the windows. He falls, rather than walks over to my side of the cabin and pulls himself into the seat next to me.

"Lee's got some control," he says through gritted teeth. "But she's not going to stay up. Hold on, it's going to be rough."

Through the windows on the other side of the copter I keep seeing alternate views of trees then clouds as we buck across the sky. My feet are pressed against the floor, my back against the seat, hopelessly trying to find solid ground. I don't know what to do with myself. I'm rigid with fear. I glance at Sherman and he's pale. This isn't something that's happened to him before either.

I turn to look out of my own window behind me. The trees are close now, I can make out leaves in their dense, dark green foliage. I wonder where we're going to land.

Suddenly, there's a tremendous jolt, a moment of free fall, then another jolt and time slows down.

For what seems like forever there is nothing but metallic shrieks and crashes and we're violently flung from side to side and up and down and I'm being pushed and pulled every which way, held in only by my harness. It feels like a giant hand is shaking and shaking us.

Suddenly it's over. Somewhere in the chaos, the engine stopped and now there is complete silence and complete stillness.

I'm hanging in my harness. We must be on an angle and my legs are in space.

Sherman unclips and drops to the floor, sliding down it to the join between the floor and the opposite wall. He climbs up to the cockpit, stepping awkwardly over the dead pilot, who is now sprawling at an awkward angle half across the doorway, half across the wall. He pulls himself in, then is back in an instant. Shock on his face.

"We've got to find Lee," is all he says, then he goes to the side door and he's wrenching and wrenching on it. It's jammed.

"What's happened?" I ask.

He's still pulling on the door, so I unbuckle and fall to the floor, landing badly. I clamber up into the cockpit too afraid of even touching the dead pilot. A glance inside tells me what's happened: half of it is gone. The nose of the copter has sheared off in the crash and the pilots' seats – and Lee and the other pilot with them – are no longer there.

[5]

I TURN BACK TO SHERMAN and he's found the manual override for the door and is cranking it open. As soon as it's wide enough for him, he jumps out. I follow.

The copter has come to a stop against two trees which are tilted at an angle, leaning against neighboring trees. Behind us is a trail of destruction. Trees have been toppled, branches have been ripped from their trunks. The copter's tail has gone. I can see it bent around a tree a hundred yards back. I follow where I assume Sherman has gone, tripping over branches. Where's Lee? My heart is in my mouth.

We find the nose section. The other pilot's seat has been half torn out and is on its side. I don't know if that pilot had been alive before, but I don't think he is now. Lee's seat has gone, assuming he was even in a seat.

"Lee!" shouts Sherman. I join in. I don't know why we're shouting. If he's dead, he can't hear us. How can he be dead?

I think I see a rock at first, but no, it's the seat, the bottom of the seat. Then I see the legs. It's him. I stumble over.

The seat is lying on its back on a mass of smaller branches that could have provided some kind of cushioning.

Sherman is right behind me.

"He's breathing!" I say.

Then Lee opens his eyes. He offers a dazed frown.

"We make it?" he croaks.

He makes to unbuckle himself.

"Wait while I check you over," says Sherman.

He bends down and feels down Lee's body. I know he's feeling for broken bones or swelling.

"Am I all there?" says Lee.

"Seem to be," says Sherman. He unclips the harness and eases Lee up.

"Mouse made it too," he smiles at me. "Good job it was you not her," he says. "Blueblood bones are much stronger." Then he turns back to Lee. "Do you know where we are?"

Lee shakes his head.

"A compass would be a start," he says.

Sherman nods.

"Then let's see what we can get from the copter."

Sherman bends and puts his shoulder under his brother, slowly standing up. He supports him back to the copter. As we reach it, Lee pulls away and stands on his own for a moment, seemingly testing the sensation.

I leap up into the copter's main cabin, filled with an urge to do something useful. The brothers have put their jackets on now and I find mine. Now the initial shock has gone, I'm noticing how much colder it is this far north.

Most of the supplies are still tied down on their pallets, but a couple have come loose. I start to unclip the cases. In the first I find ration packs. They're labelled 'Stew: beef and vegetable'. I look at a few and all of them are the same. So we won't starve before we make it to the base. I look in another. More rations. 'Rice: chow mein' it says. At least there's some variety.

Lee has come in now. He's opening one of a number of long thin crates. I suspect he knew what was in it. There are two rifles in each one, matt black and mean looking in their foam packing. He eases one out and ratchets on something. There's a sliding sound and I pull back instinctively. He glances at me.

"Not loaded," he says. Then he goes to another case, a squarer one. He unscrews the latch and opens that. There are long, square, black cartridges inside. He takes one out and snaps it into a slot on the rifle.

"Now it is," he says.

Sherman joins us. He gathers up our kit bags.

"We should just take what we need out of these. I don't suppose there's a comms unit amongst that lot?"

"Not that I've found yet."

"We've got food and guns," I say.

"There's a compass in my bag's side pocket," says Lee. "Start plotting a course how we can get out of here. Do you have a nav system?"

"Only my tab," says Sherman. "And that's not military grade. I doubt it'll tell us anything we don't already know."

We rummage around a bit more and pretty soon we've rustled up a fair bit of gear. Lee has taken command. He doles out ten days of ration packs. He and Sherman have both armed themselves with a pistol and a rifle and have stuffed their packs with ammunition. They've given me a pistol too. It's surprisingly heavy and I'm glad they haven't tried to give me a rifle as well. We also each have a spare set of underwear, a flashlight, a compass, an emergency blanket, bivouac tarp, stove.

Once we're packed, it's the first time I've had a moment to think before the world went crazy. My familiar bed this morning seems like weeks away. Part of me can't believe I'm here, can't believe what's happened to me today.

While the terror of the crash is behind me, the wreckage is a constant reminder of how close we came. So are the two bodies covered with emergency blankets and lying over by the fuselage. That could so easily have been us. Been me. It's too much for me to take in. I get up and start walking.

"Where are you going?"

It's Lee. Nice of him to notice me, even if his voice sounds suspicious.

"I need a walk."

"Don't go far."

He must think I'm stupid. I've never been out of the city. The biggest forest I've been in was one of the groves in a city park. I walk out of the semi clearing our crash made. The brothers start to talk.

"I've plotted out where I think the base is," says Lee, "but I think we should stay put."

This conversation is only meant for his brother of course. I'm an irrelevance. I step into the trees.

"We can either try to get there ourselves," he continues, "or we can wait here for them to come and find us."

"Wouldn't it be better to meet them half way?" asks Sherman.

"Our maps aren't good enough in this terrain. We've got a high chance of getting lost. I think we should wait. They'll have seen us come down."

"Are you sure? Why did you make us pack bags then?"

"In case we need to get away quickly."

"Why would we need to do that?"

"We were taken out by ground fire, remember. We don't know where those Rads are."

I look around. Suddenly the forest doesn't seem so quiet, so benign. My ears have always been sharp and the forest is so quiet compared to the city, I think I'll probably hear anything.

I inhale. Smells of foliage and damp earth fill my nostrils. It's beautiful, so clean compared to the city. And there is birdsong too. I can't see them yet, but I can pick out several different calls somewhere up in the trees. Birds aren't new to me; there are plenty in the city living on the edges of what people leave behind, but I don't remember hearing them singing. To me, the sound of the city is traffic, human voices and the hum of technology. It's the absence of that hum that I notice most, the noise that's always there and leaves a big gap when it disappears.

I walk deeper into the forest. It seems to draw me in. I see the moss on the trees. It's mainly on one side of them. Plants grow on anything. The ground is soft and giving under my feet. I would have expected just dirt between the trees, but there is moss there too, ground cover and bushes and years of fallen leaves and broken, half rotted branches.

There are mushrooms, sometimes in clusters, others a solitary, bright cap. They look good enough to eat, but we get mushrooms in the city too and every street kid knows that, while some are good, others can poison you. I learned a few in the city, but I don't recognize any of these.

Something snaps and my head whips around, my heart suddenly pumping fast. I scan through the trees, but see just trunks receding into the dimness of the deeper forest. Then my eye catches a movement. It's some kind of animal, a short brown creature, nuzzling amongst the leaves. Don't ask me what it is. I just know it's not a fox or a dog. I relax, but it's still put me on edge. I keep looking around me now and I decide to wander back to the others to see what they've decided.

"What's happening?" I ask as I emerge from the trees. Lee is back inside the copter, rooting out anything useful. Sherman has brought another case outside and is going through it, spreading things on the ground next to him. So far, it just seems to be machine parts.

"We're staying put for now," says Sherman.

That suits me. The forest is so big. From the air, it went on and on with only a few lakes to break it up. The copter, wreck as it is, feels like an island in a sea of trees. It gives us shelter of a sort and more supplies than we can carry. Still, I hear disappointment in Sherman's voice.

"You don't seem happy about that," I say.

"Well yeah, it's the sensible thing to do," he says. He puts an emphasis on the word 'sensible' making it sound like the stupid thing to do. "But I just hate sitting still. I feel like I'm not doing anything, I feel like I'm making someone else do all the work for me. We're soldiers aren't we? We take the initiative."

"I don't know, it seems like a good idea to me."

He looks at me with a sneer.

"And what would you know?"

I'm taken aback.

"Nothing, I suppose. I'm just a redblood domestic."

I see I've made an impact and decide to leave it at that.

We use the stove to cook some dinner. We polish off beef stew and what Lee calls combat cookies. These are chewie bars which seem designed to give you something to do as much as providing nourishment.

"Shouldn't the base have sent a copter by now?" I ask.

From the looks I get, I think I've hit a raw nerve. Sherman gives Lee a meaningful look.

"There's lots of forest to cover," says Lee. "They probably didn't get a clear fix on where we came down."

"So how long can we expect?"

Lee looks uncomfortable.

"Another forty-eight hours before we see anything. It depends how many aircraft they've got spare to cover a standard search grid."

"He's just making it up," Sherman mutters to me. Lee scowls at him.

"We need to give them a chance to find us," Lee says with measured calm.

The sun appears briefly out of the cloud and for a moment, a golden green light flows around us, but then it's snuffed out as cloud or trees reclaim the sun again. Almost immediately the air turns chill.

"We'll take turns on watch. I'll take first. Muswell, you're next."

So I can be useful at last.

Sure enough, Lee wakes me. To my surprise, I've been sleeping deeply and it takes me a few moments to recognize where I am. I'm shocked all over again.

He hands me his watch and I get up and leave the copter, taking a blanket with me. I pull it around me and find Lee's made himself a seat out of crates with something to lean against. I sit and listen to the night. It's full of sounds: croaks, creaks and chirrups, and a low swishing which I assume is the leaves in a breeze which I can't feel down here on the ground.

I've got plenty of time to think.

I'm surprised to find I'm glad Lee's here as well as Sherman. He's more experienced and his cooler head is needed in this situation. Both of them are out of their depth though. Maybe anyone would be.

Something is snuffling around on the edge of our clearing. I pull the pistol out of my holster and rest it on my knee. Its cold weight is reassuring even if I'm pretty clueless about how to use it. I toy with the safety catch, unable to decide whether to turn it off so I'm ready as I don't trust myself to remember if something happens. I don't know what that something would be, but my imagination is supplying everything from ambush to dinosaurs.

A clear bird call sounds from the trees and keeps repeating. It's a long whistle on two notes. I think it's an owl. I hope it's an owl.

I remember the signal whistles I used to use when I was on the street. We would scavenge for out of date food in dumpsters behind foodmarts and restaurants. We ate well when we did that, but the police knew about them too and would patrol them regularly to catch vagrants. Rat catchers we called them. It was a term they accepted with pride.

I shiver and hunker down into the seat. Although my eyes have become accustomed to the darkness, there's still little light.

There are no stars: I can just make out the cloud covering them. The forest seems threatening now. It could be hiding anything or anyone.

Although I can only see its edges, I can sense the whole mass of life. It closes in around us.

I try to breathe quietly so that I can still hear anything else, but it takes me a while to become used to the natural night sounds of the forest.

Even so, it is peaceful sitting here. And they've let me do something useful, even if it is just to give them a break. Maybe it's a measure of how safe Lee feels.

I make a conscious effort to breathe deeply: in through my nose, out through my mouth. It's calming. I even smile to myself. This morning I was a domestic in the city. Tonight I have more independence than I've ever had before, even if I am lost in the forest in a northern night. For the first time in years, I've no idea what the morning might bring, but for now I'll enjoy this moment of calm, this chance to work equally with the blueblood brothers.

With that changed mindset, I'm surprised when Lee's watch beeps to tell me it's time for me to wake Sherman. I go and shake him. He's reluctant to wake up, but when he does, he peers up at me. I can see his eyes.

"Hey Mouse. What are you doing in my bedroom?"

"Trying to get some sleep. Hurry up, before something creeps up on us."

"I love it when you're forceful," he whispers. Then he pulls himself up and brushes past.

I pull a couple of blankets over me and rest my head on my bag. I don't remember lying awake for long. I remember waking up though.

I wake suddenly to a bang and a shout. I leap up confused, my heart pumping and my head still trying to work out what's going on.

[6]

SOMEONE IS SHOUTING AND LEE is rushing past me with a gun.

"Get down! It's Rads!" he says.

He positions himself next to the open door and peers carefully around the opening. Sherman must still be outside. I drop to the deck and peer around the edge of a window. It's on the side of the tilted copter which is close to the ground. Sure enough, Sherman is out there. He's lying down behind the seat of cases which is giving him some cover and looking out into the trees. I can't see anything out there.

"Take a look out back," says Lee.

I'm almost afraid to move, but I crawl around and reach for the bench on the other side of the copter which is above me. I pull myself up to it and look through the window. I see movement immediately, but I'm so shocked, I let go and drop back.

"There's someone out there."

"How many?" demands Lee.

"I don't know. At least two or three."

He curses.

"Sherm, they're behind us too," he hisses.

Lee looks at the cockpit, hesitates for a moment, then dives across the open doorway. There's an instant blast of gunfire which dings off the fuselage. It's returned immediately by Sherman, but Lee has reached the cockpit door unscathed. He's still crouching. He's got some kind of view of the other side through the blown off nose. He lifts his rifle to his shoulder and watches, then he pulls the trigger. Once, twice, a pause, then a third time.

A blast of gunfire rakes the front of the copter and Lee pulls away from the open cockpit doorway. I cower on the floor, my hands over my head. I feel so helpless, so trapped in this damn wreck.

"Did you get anyone?" I ask. I can barely speak.

"Maybe," says Lee.

I don't know if he was going to say any more, but there's more firing from out front. It stops abruptly from Sherman's side.

I can hear Sherman's muttered curse. Lee rolls his eyes. I know what it is: Sherman's out of ammunition. We wait for him to reload, but all we hear is another curse. I look at Sherman's backpack by his blankets. It's still buckled and I can see the outline of several magazines on an outside pocket. He doesn't have any more ammunition.

Lee peers out the front again, lifting his weapon. Gunshots ring out from behind us too. I can hear them hitting inside the cockpit. Lee cries out and falls back, his rifle dropping from his hand. He's holding his shoulder. My eyes widen.

"Are you okay?"

"I'm hit," he says.

"Throw your weapons down!" comes a voice from outside.

Lee looks wildly at the door. I can tell he's trying to work out what to do.

"Throw out your weapons, then you follow with your hands on your head. We've got a boomer so we can end this bigtime if that's how you want it."

I don't know what a boomer is, but Lee does. He throws his gun out the door and follows it with his pistol.

"We're coming out," he says. "There are two of us in here."

I look at him, but he doesn't meet my eyes. As I stand up, I feel the weight of the pistol in my belt. I pull it out and throw it at the door. It's an awkward throw and it bounces off the door frame, teeters on the step for a moment, then drops onto the ground. Lee steps tentatively into the opening.

"We see ya. Come on out, slowly."

Lee does as they say and I can no longer see him. Then it's my turn. I put my hands on my head and go slowly to the door. I need a pee so bad right now. I can see Lee again. He's looking wobbly on his feet. Sherman is standing as well and he reaches out to support his brother. There's blood on the front of his shirt.

"Sorry," says Sherman. "I wasn't expecting them."

Even I know that's a stupid excuse, although I didn't take any spare magazines with me when I was on watch either. It just didn't occur to me.

I step out of the copter and move to stand next to the brothers. I still can't see any of our attackers.

"If that's not all of you, we'll shoot all three of you, understand?" says the voice from the trees.

"That's all of us," says Lee, his voice is quiet. He's ashamed and angry.

"Cool," says the voice.

Then I see its owner. He steps out from one of the trees. He has a gun leaning casually over his shoulder and he strolls up to us. He oozes confidence. He is wearing faded olive green combat gear which has seen better days. His hair is short yet ragged and there's several days' stubble on his chin. He's not as tall as Lee, but he looks a few years older, mid-twenties maybe, and his eyes are older still. They're a pale grey-blue and hypnotizing. He nods his head in approval of something, possibly himself.

"Looks like we bagged ourselves some Blues," he says. Then he saunters past us and looks inside the copter. I turn to watch him. He looks back at us.

"And it is indeed just the three of you."

"You killed the pilots," I say, surprising myself as much as him. He smiles and comes over.

"Sorry about that," he says. "They were making a mess of my sky. But it's good to see you've brought me some presents to make up for it."

Lee sinks to the ground. We go to help him.

"Leave him," says the man and moves over to him.

"And how are you?" he asks with false sincerity. "Are you going to need any help or are you going to fix yourself up Mr Blue? If you are blueblood."

None of us says anything and he bends down and inspects Lee's jacket.

Lee is watching him with a fierce frown on his face, but he says nothing. The Rad carefully peels back the jacket. Lee keeps watching him and the man is watching Lee's face carefully too. I would have expected that to hurt, but Lee is taking it well. Then I realize his nanomeds have probably anaesthetized the area.

"Shoulder. You should live."

Then the man does a strange thing. He reaches out and places a finger in Lee's blood, lifts it to his mouth and licks it. His eyes search the air and he's clearly savoring it, thinking. Then he nods.

"And all the faster with activated nanomeds. We'll get you comfortable."

He straightens and inspects Sherman.

"What?" he says. "Are you guys so short of manpower that you're sending cadets into battle now?"

He looks down at Lee as if it's his fault.

"Fancy sending a boy to a man's war."

We still haven't seen any more of his unit, although we know they're out there, but now he raises his voice and calls to them.

"Come on out. Bring Virge."

They appear from all over our clearing. There's an even dozen of them, but one is being supported by one of the others. This must be Virge. The biggest of them is carrying what I take to be a missile launcher over his shoulder. I assume that is the boomer the man talked about.

They are all dressed in a similar fashion to the first one who appears to be their leader, but none are dressed the same and there appears to be no formal uniform. I must admit, while they don't look smart, they do look effective, not least because of their obvious discipline. They also look like they've seen a good deal of action. They range from maybe Lee's age to much older, perhaps forties, but this man is clearly the one in charge. He has the charisma of a leader.

Now he stands and looks at the two of us.

"Get him cleaned up."

Sherman makes to turn around, but the man raises a finger at him and his eyes flash.

"But nothing funny."

[7]

WE FETCH A MEDICAL KIT and get to work. We carefully peel back Lee's clothes, adding sterilized water where they're sticking to his wound. I hold a flashlight while Sherman probes carefully. He's looking for bone fragments and clothing, but his movements are clumsy in the small area of the wound.

"Let me do it," I say and he lets me. I take the tweezers. It's a strange feeling probing inside torn flesh that belongs to a human.

"How's it looking, Nurse Mouse?" Sherman asks in a low voice.

The bullet has hit Lee's collar bone and passed through his shoulder, leaving a larger exit wound.

"I've seen worse," I tell him. Sometimes the police would shoot at us even though most of us were only kids. Maybe they were just trying to scare us because they usually missed, but sometimes someone would get hit. If they did, we didn't have much we could do to help them, but a bullet in a kid makes a pretty big hole. That's what they think of vagrants. We're the lowest of the low.

I pick out what I can find. Lee watches me quietly. I feel his eyes on me. I look at him and he looks away. We have to turn him over so I can inspect both the entry and exit wounds. I get out what I can.

"What can we do about this collar bone? All I can think of is to put him a sling. We can't strap it."

Sherman shakes his head and rummages in the medical kit, pulling out a roll of tape.

"What is it?"

"Bone tape. It'll hold the two ends together while they mend. The nanomeds will dissolve it when they don't need it."

He wants me to wrap it around. This is going to be difficult. I keep being surprised that Lee is taking this so calmly.

"Can't you feel this?" I ask.

"I can feel you pushing me around, but it doesn't hurt."

With Sherman's help, I get the two ends of bone pointing at each other and wrap the tape around them. Passing it underneath is difficult. I'm glad I'm wearing medical gloves because they're covered in Lee's blood.

Just for a moment, I pause to look at it, remembering how the Rad leader licked it. He's behind me now.

"All done?" he asks.

I nod.

"Don't cover it yet. Sit him up."

We lean Lee against the cases Sherman had been trying to hide behind. The man looks behind him.

"Hey Virge, they're ready for you. Come get your medicine."

Virge picks himself up unsteadily and comes over. He kneels down next to Sherman, then leans across him and sticks out his tongue.

"No!" Lee and I shout together in disgust.

"Quiet!" the leader barks, unslinging his rifle from his shoulder. Then he says more quietly to Virge. "Not your tongue. Your whole mouth. Suck it up."

Virge does as he's told. He opens his whole mouth and covers the wound with it. I can hear him sucking.

"What are you doing?" says Lee. He's seething and trying to pull away, but he's stuck against the crates.

The leader smiles.

"Getting some of your nanomeds. He picked up a bit of dysentery. They should sort him out."

Virge leans back. There's blood around his mouth. Lee's blood. It's disgusting.

"That enough?" he asks.

"We'll see. You can always come back for more if it's not. We've got ourselves some cows."

"Thanks Julius," says Virge and he stands up and goes back to lean on the fuselage.

"We'll need to clean that again," I say.

The Rad leader frowns at me.

"Only if you want to."

He looks at Sherman, then back to me again.

"You don't know do you?" he asks.

"What?" I'm trying to sound fierce.

"I'll show you," he says while two of his men come over and wrap plastic restraints around Sherman's wrists.

"Give me your hand," he says to me. He says it gently, but it's a command.

I don't move, so he takes my hand and pulls it up. I'm looking him straight in the eye. They're amazing eyes. The pupils stand out from the irises which are a clear grey-blue. He is holding my hand firmly, yet gently.

Looking into his eyes, I don't notice him produce a knife until it's next to my hand. Quickly he opens my fingers and runs the blade over my pinkie. I cry out and blood seeps from the cut. He puts my finger in his mouth. It's an oddly sensual thing to do. He is still looking me straight in the eye. There is curiosity in them. He's inspecting me.

He takes my finger out of his mouth, but keeps hold of my hand. He's tasting again. Then he smiles.

"You're one of us aren't you? You're redblood."

One of them. I hadn't thought of it being like that, but that is what the Rads are, redbloods who want to overturn society as it's run by bluebloods. I don't see any point in denying my bloodline. Surely that's not a military secret.

"Yes, I'm redblood."

I can feel Sherman's and Lee's eyes on me. Something has changed. Last night, I was their domestic and they were in charge. Now they're no longer in charge, redbloods are. So what does that make me?

Julius looks away. I miss his eyes.

"You can dress his wound now."

I kneel down again and take a dressing from the medkit. Before I put it on, I clean the wound where Virge had his mouth.

"I should give you a jab as well," I say.

"No need," says Sherman. "The nanomeds will have it covered."

I shrug. "If you say so."

I place the dressing over the wound and smooth it down. I fetch him a clean shirt and jacket from his bag and help him put them on.

"Thank you," he mutters.

I lean over him to help put his arm in the sleeve on the injured side. He inhales deeply as I do it.

"Sorry, did that hurt?" I ask.

"No," he says. "It's okay."

I straighten up his clothes and check for blood seeping through the dressing.

"Don't trust them," he says suddenly, whispering.

"What?"

"You may be a redblood like them, but you're not like them."

"How come?" I ask.

"They want what they can't have. You don't."

"Are you quite sure of that?" I ask. Maybe I shouldn't have said it, but I'm emboldened by seeing him powerless.

[8]

I LEAVE SHERMAN AND GO and sit on my own.

Julius comes over and sits next to me.

"Mind if I take a seat?" he asks. He has a friendly smile.

"Go ahead," I say, although he's already sat down.

"So what are you to them? Servant or whore?"

The abruptness of the question takes my breath away. One thing I'll give the Hammond boys, they always behaved around me.

"I work for their family," I say.

"Aah," he says, as if understanding something quite different from what I meant. I feel further explanation is necessary.

"You might call me a domestic, but I help out with anything around their property."

"I see. So what then were you doing on a military copter?"

"Is this an interrogation?"

He laughs. "Hardly. I'd rather call it curiosity in action. I find asking questions helps you find out things you don't know."

"I've found that too. I also find trial and error useful."

"Yeah. But out here, trial and error isn't much good if the error leaves you dead."

"Sherman wanted me to go with him to be his attendant."

"So the rich boy wanted someone to press his uniform for him?"

"I suppose."

"And which one's Sherman?"

Part of me feels I've given away too much already, but then again, it's just his name.

"The one you cuffed."

"The cadet? Well, well. He really does have ideas above his station doesn't he?" He looks over at Sherman, then over at the wreck of the copter. "So how do you like your new situation?" he asks. "You never made it up there did you?"

"Where?"

"No need to be coy. You're obviously heading for Borealis Base because there's nothing else up here, at least nothing else up here where they'd send this copter directly. I could tell from the direction you were flying that you hadn't been there yet. So I'll ask you again. How do you like your new situation?"

"Different," I say. It's kind of hard to explain how I feel right now, surrounded by armed men in the woods miles from anywhere.

He leaps up and spreads his arms out.

"Don't you feel free?"

He says it loudly and with a big smile. Sherman and Lee both look over and frown. I feel self-conscious.

"I did last night. This morning I've been captured by men with guns and I don't know what's going to happen next."

He throws his head back and laughs.

"What's your name?"

"Mouse."

He smiles again. It is easy and open. He's very likeable when he smiles, if only the situation were different. He crouches in front of me and extends his hand.

"Pleased to meet you, Mouse. I'm Julius."

I shake his hand tentatively, very aware that Sherman and Lee are watching me and wondering what they're thinking.

"How about this, Mouse? I hereby free you from your servitude. Out here, we're all vagrants and the police find it a lot harder to find us. And sometimes rather costly."

"Thanks," I say. "So what does that mean? I'm free to go?"

He has a free and open laugh.

"Of course. But it's probably not a good idea to go anywhere on your own. You could get lost or eaten by a bear."

"There are bears?"

"Yes. And wolves and cougars. But it's the ones from over the mountains that you better watch out for. The radiation did something to them and made them wilder. Added to that are the mutations and the toxins. It all passes down to their offspring, concentrating with each generation. You can tell because most wolves will only attack you if they feel threatened. West coast ones will attack you just because you're there."

He swiftly undoes his jacket and pulls it off his left side, exposing it to the cold air. The first thing I notice is how toned his torso is. The second thing I notice is the parallel paler lines of scarring across his shoulder.

"See? I had a little run in with a grizzly. Fortunately it was a young one and I happened to have my pistol in my right hand."

"Sounds lucky."

"Mostly, although I am a little radioactive now. So I take a little blueblood when I can to see if it helps."

"Is that what you – what Virge – was doing before?" I ask.

"Yeah, and why not? They just got the nanomeds because they can. So we take them when we can."

"I've heard of them giving it to redblood employees they like. I've never heard of anyone taking it. Does it still work?"

"Of course. But not for long. It doesn't get far out of the digestive system. We need a way to get it into the bloodstream. Then we'd be the same as them."

"So Virge was trying to cure his dysentery with Lee's blood?"

"If that's his name. Yep. Seen it work before."

In my mind, I see it again as Virge clamps his mouth to Lee's shoulder. I shudder. It was wild and animal.

"You should try it. You could now."

I know I'm looking horrified.

"It's the only thing between us," he continues. "They think they're better than us just because they've got little machines. Well, they came out of human ingenuity and technology's for everyone. That's what we're going to change."

"I just thought the Rads want to live free."

"We do!" His eyes are wide and animated. "But free doesn't mean hunted in a forest picking off the Blues from behind trees. I want my freedom to be something more than fighting a war. If we take what's ours by right, if we all get nanomeds, we become free and we gain peace, because then we're all the same."

I stare off into space. If my mother or my aunt had had nanomeds, I bet they wouldn't be dead now. I'd have a family and a home. We would all have what we wanted: the same health as the bluebloods, longer lives. We would have hope. This isn't what I've heard about the Rads before through the live-stream. Maybe this is just Julius' view.

"Just think of the possibilities?" he continues. "The nanomeds they're making now don't just cure the carrier, they improve the carrier. They're giving people abilities they never had before. Pretty soon, people will be able to reclaim the West Coast. All that crap over there won't mean anything." His eyes are shining.

"Won't that make you less human?"

"Does wearing an aqualung underwater make you less human?"

"You can take off an aqualung. The nanos are in you for life."

"Oh they can be flushed out with the right equipment, but why would you want to? If we all had this technology, imagine the advances we could make. There's nothing we couldn't do."

He turns towards the brothers. They're pretending they're not watching us, but I can tell they are.

"But if they won't give it to us," he says. "We've just got to take it."

He gets up and walks back to the copter. Some of his men are going through all the supplies.

Sherman and Lee exchange a comment. Lee shakes his head.

I don't know why I feel like I'm betraying them.

[9]

AFTER JULIUS LEAVES, I stay sitting on my own for a while, thinking about what he told me. I used to think the Rads wanted out, that they just wanted to overturn the status quo. But now, if what Julius says is typical of the whole movement, it seems they want *in*.

I can't get my head past the blood-sucking thing. It seemed so primitive, so bestial. I need to talk this over with someone and the only people I have to talk to are Lee and Sherman. I know there's been a power shift and I don't know how long this can continue. I can only assume Borealis Base is searching for us and with their superior technology, they should be able to find us. But then again, if it were that easy, Julius and his team would all have been dead long ago. So things are very uncertain.

I try to put myself into the shoes of Lee and Sherman. If I'm confused and afraid, they, as bluebloods, must be feeling just as disorientated.

They may not be my social equals, but I've known them for years and that means something. They've generally been good to me, or at least, not bad, which amounts to the same thing if you've heard some of the stories and seen some of the things I have. They're the closest thing to family that I've got. No, that's not quite true. Grandad is the closest thing I have to family. I miss him right now. He's the one I want to be talking to. He's got wisdom and experience to call on. The three of us have got instincts or training. My guess is I'm better at the former, but the boys have got the latter.

I rejoin them. They've been talking quietly. Sherman is still cuffed. They haven't restrained Lee except to tie his ankle to a post which has been stuck in the ground near him.

"Ah, you've come back to us," says Sherman. There's half a smile on his face, but Lee looks sullen.

"How are you guys?" I ask.

"Nice of you to show an interest," Sherman replies. "Your blood-sucking friends have been good to us. We're still alive, although how long for, I don't know."

"They're not my friends."

"You seemed pretty chummy to us."

"He was just talking to me about what they want."

"Do you know why they tried to eat me?" says Lee.

"He was trying to get your nanomeds. The man's got dysentery."

Lee frowns and rolls his eyes at the same time.

"They're just animals!"

"It is pretty weird. But that's all they want. They just want access to the nanomed technology."

"They don't deserve it. Look how inferior they are."

"Thank you," I say sarcastically. He gets my meaning.

"You've lived with us for years."

"Then thank you for rescuing my from my primitive existence."

He scowls again.

"Mouse," says Sherman. "Can you help us get away?"

"Is that a good idea?" I say.

"Now it's going to be my turn to be sarcastic."

"We're in the middle of the forest. Where are you going to go?"

"Borealis Base of course. We were going to get there on our own before."

"But how will you survive?"

"You'd help us get supplies and weapons."

"That's a big ask."

"Redbloods trust redbloods. You seem to have the run of the camp."

"Don't count on it."

Now I'm really confused. For years I've not really questioned what I've seen on the live-stream. I went along with the government's view that the Rads were just anarchists and terrorists. But now, I realize I want what they want. On the other hand, it's so unlikely that it will happen. I need to look after the Hammonds. They're the only thing between me and vagrancy. I don't think I could bear to lose it all again. I'm also scared. Helping the brothers would be very dangerous. It could get us all killed.

"Shouldn't you wait until the army find us?" I say.

"That could take days," says Lee.

"You were pretty confident about it yesterday."

"This isn't getting us anywhere," says Sherman.

I stare sullenly at the ground. I'm angry because I'm frightened. They're asking me to do something dangerous. They see me as the loyal servant. That's good. That means the work I've done for the last six years hasn't been for nothing. It means I might just be working towards the kind of status Mrs Hunter has. I don't know whether to be grateful or disgusted. Disgusted with myself even. Everything I've done in my life has been to help me, directly or indirectly. The streets taught me about survival, about using my wits and learning fast. I know I could use those out here.

"Could you just look for an opportunity?" Lee asks.

"Okay," I say. It doesn't commit me to anything. It seems to be enough reassurance for now.

We watch Julius and his unit stripping the supplies and anything else useful out of the wreck of the copter. Most of the supplies have survived the crash. Some of these they empty into their own packs, particularly the food. The rest they stack onto sleds which they build out of pieces of fuselage, using the flattest pieces of metal as the base. They attach webbing and use it to pull them along the forest floor. Sometimes they catch on a stump or plant, but they move enough over the roots and leaf litter.

All of this is accomplished by early afternoon. During this time, I've left Sherman and Lee a few times. I've been watching the Rads working and helping each other. They're a jokey bunch. Most of them have nicknames. The big guy with the boomer is called Double, and the one who helps Virge is Hornet. There's also Stubble, Rash and Eames. There's a girl too, Livia. She has the same eyes as Julius. I think they might be brother and sister.

I'm impressed by their ingenuity, making good use of the few tools that they found and quickly building serviceable trays on which they can carry out the supplies.

No one says much to me, but they're all friendly enough. Actually, it's more I don't talk to them. Most of them greet me. The only unfriendly one is Rash. He has a lean, wild face and a shaved head. He looks at me like he doesn't trust me, which I suppose is fair enough. Maybe he's the smart one. I wouldn't know whether to trust me either.

Julius is supervising selecting the supplies for the sleds.

"Shall we burn the rest?" asks the one called Stubble. I don't know why he's called Stubble; he's got the longest beard.

"No," says Julius. "It would make too much smoke. Just leave a beacon on it."

He walks over to us.

"On your feet. We're moving out."

"Where are we going?" Lee asks.

Julius raises a quizzical eyebrow.

"Now what would you tell me if you were in my shoes?"

The unit forms up. There's someone out front and two people pulling each of the four sleds. Everyone is carrying a heavy pack. They've even given ones to us. Sherman's looks heavier than everyone else's because he's not carrying weapons. Lee gets a lighter one because of his shoulder. So do I, but that's more likely because I'd disappear under a full military backpack.

For a while, walking through the trees makes a welcome change to sitting by the wrecked copter. After a few hours, I don't notice the pack as much, although it's still a relief when we take breaks. I don't take it off though. I tried that the first time we had a break, but air cooled the sweat on my back and chilled me. It's much warmer when we're walking.

We stash two of the sleds as we're going. One is in a cleft of a rocky outcrop, another is on top of a small hill which has a view over the surrounding country.

Just like the view from the copter, there seems to be little but trees here. There are other hills like the one we're on and rocky crags. I can get my bearings because I can see the mountains, or the base of them at least. Their tops are covered in cloud. So it doesn't take much to work out which direction we're going because we're going roughly towards them. West.

We have a short rest at each of the sled drops. I try to take a look at Lee's dressing, but he shrugs me off and makes a point of asking Sherman to do it instead.

We make faster progress with four men to a sled. They're not easy to drag through the trees, so it helps to have more people available to unsnag them when they get stuck.

It's getting dark when we stop for the night. The unit spreads out among the trees. Lee watches them more closely than Sherman. I can see him thinking

"Do I need to tie you to anything?"

I jump. I didn't hear Julius approach.

"How long have you known them?" he asks me.

"More than six years."

"Long enough, I'm afraid. You look very friendly with each other."

"That's what they're saying about you and me too."

"Mouse in the middle," he says. He's studying me. "I think I'd better tie you to something."

I'm relieved. Not only does it take away my ability to help Sherman and Lee escape, but it might show them I'm not so trusted by the Rads.

Even as I think that, I wonder why that's important to me. Julius is right: I am Mouse in the middle. I don't know what to think. Not knowing what's going on isn't helping and I resent having no control over things. It's worse than working for the Hammonds. At least there I could usually decide what I did next.

[10]

THE RADS RIG UP BIVOUACS under the trees for us and we wrap up in bedrolls and blankets. The ground is hard, but I'm reasonably warm. Last night in the copter, I could only smell the metal and the engine fumes. Out here, I'm closer to forest and the rich, damp smell that comes up from the ground. I like it. It smells good. I breathe it in deeply and after all the exercise of the afternoon, sleep comes quickly.

Everyone is up early. Breakfast is eaten while we are packing everything away. Virge comes over and grins at Lee.

"Feeling so much better today," he says, chuckling. "Not sure I'll need any more of you this time!"

Lee just stares at him, doing the silent tough guy bit. It doesn't seem to impress Virge who goes away again, still chuckling.

"Could the nanomeds really do that just from sucking them out?" I ask.

Sherman shrugs. "Don't know much about them, but we probably wouldn't catch dysentery in the first place."

The day is much like yesterday: constant walking through the trees. There's little wildlife to see. I suppose it's frightened off by us, although we're quiet enough. Most of the sound comes from Sherman and Lee. I can't tell if they're doing it to irritate our captors or because they can't help it.

It's after our lunch break when one of them, Singer I think his name is, raises a hand for us to halt. He's looking at a device hanging around his neck and wearing headphones. Julius goes up to see what's wrong.

"Aircraft," he says. "From the size, I think it's a drone."

"They've got tab radar!" Sherman says in hushed surprise to Lee. Lee just frowns and nods, like he does.

"Spread out everyone," Julius says and the Rads obey, vanishing into different directions. Then he pulls out his pistol and points it at the brothers. "Just keep still."

A minute later, I hear a quiet buzzing. It sounds like a bee might do on the other side of a room. I look up through the leaves, but they are too thick to see through. I suppose this is a good thing, and then think about that thought. That suggests I don't want to be found, that I don't want to be rescued. Or is it just that an eye in the sky makes me feel like prey? I never did like being hunted.

The buzzing fades, but we stay still for long minutes after it has passed. Julius watches Singer who is glued to his tab. Eventually he gives a thumbs up. Julius whistles and the unit regathers and we're on our way again.

By the end of the day, all of the sleds have been stashed and we're making better progress without them to slow us down, although everyone is still laden with supplies themselves: food, weapons and ammunition. They have given more to Lee. He now has a full backpack because he's improved quickly.

Julius falls in with me.

"Ever been out of the city much?" he says.

"No. I visited a few farms on the outskirts a couple of times."

"So never been in the wild?"

I shake my head.

"Nearest thing was city park woodland."

"Hardly the same thing. They keep those nice and tidy with manicured trails." He spreads his arms out, taking in all of the forest. "But all this grows how it wants to. I love it out here."

"It is beautiful, but it's noisy at night. I always thought the wild would be quiet and that it was just the cities that were noisy."

"But it's a different sound isn't it? It's not noisy, it's full of life!"

We walk in silence for a while. I want to talk to him, but any question I can think of sounds stupid and I don't want him to think I'm stupid. He, on the other hand, looks quite comfortable with the silence between us. I look at him out of the corner of my eye, pretending I'm looking at the trees. There's something about the way he carries himself that projects leadership. He's good looking, sure, but there's an easy confidence about his face and, yes, that's it, an intensity. When he talks to me, he's completely focused on what he is talking about and on me. I don't take this personally. I've seen him do it to everyone and especially to Livia. They seem close, making each other smile with whatever they're saying to each other.

When he asks his next question, I nearly jump because I'm lost in thought.

"Your friend Lee is making remarkable progress."

"He's certainly healing well."

"You know it's the nanomeds don't you? You saw what they did to Virge's dysentery. Now they're making short work of that shoulder wound. The bone's even rebuilt itself already. He can wear a backpack now."

"He's still got extra padding inside the strap on that side," I say.

Julius waves his hand dismissively.

"The point is, he's carrying a pack over a collar bone that was shot in half only two days ago. This is what we're dealing with Mouse. They're turning themselves into supermen. But you know what this means? It's not enough to wound one of them anymore, unless it's a redblood trooper. That doesn't take them out of the fight for long enough. We've got to kill them. We've got to make it too costly to fight us."

This sounds a bit stupid to me.

"You can't just keep killing them," I say. "There will always be more. And there are more of them than there are of you."

"Fighting in the field, yes, but more of them are redbloods than bluebloods. It's the specialists, the officers, the elite units that are blues. Besides, there are far more redbloods out there than there are bluebloods. If people like you realized your power, you would rise up straight away. Then, things would be different."

He looks at me with intensity, his eyes bright.

"I'll leave you with that," he says and stalks forward to talk to Livia. He puts his arm around her shoulder, says something to her and they both burst out laughing. He drops his arm and they continue side by side, chatting. I find myself envying their relaxed intimacy.

Around mid-morning, Singer puts up his hand again. There's another drone. Everyone scatters once more and we lie there under the leaves waiting for it to pass. But this one takes its time. It buzzes backwards and forwards and side to side.

I look at Sherman and Lee and there seems to be some wordless communication going on between them.

"What's it doing?" I whisper.

"It's running a search grid," says Lee. "It's suspicious."

Everyone is peering up through the branches. For an instant I see a black shape pass by overhead. It does seem to be coming closer. It would be hard to zero in completely because the Rads have separated, but I suppose it depends on the sensitivity of its sensors.

From the look on his face, Julius is thinking this too. The buzzing comes closer. Its flybys are increasingly short. It's homing in on somebody.

"It's found us, Julius," says Lee with more than a hint of satisfaction.

In reply, Julius waves his pistol menacingly and puts his finger to his lips.

Shorter and shorter come the beats of the buzzing.

Suddenly there are three loud cracks and we hear a cry from the trees to our right.

"It's armed! Double, take it out!" Julius shouts.

We hear the buzzing again.

"I wonder if it can tell where *you* are," Julius says meaningfully to Lee and Sherman. "Or are you in the firing line too?"

From the look on their faces, I think Sherman and Lee believe they're just as much targets as the Rads. My heart is certainly pounding.

The buzzing starts again. It is searching for new targets, coming closer to us, I'm sure of it. Perhaps it heard Julius's shout to Double and we're only a few yards from him. We're relatively bunched up compared to the rest of the Rads. What's Double doing?

The buzzing sounds like it is almost overhead.

There's a whoosh and a bang. I duck instinctively and something hits me on the shoulder. I look up. Julius is smiling and clapping. Double and a couple of the others emerge. He's also smiling and toting the boomer over his shoulder. Julius picks up a lump of metal that must have come from the downed drone and lobs it at the feet of Lee.

"Yours, I believe," he says.

Then there's a shout from amongst the trees. Julius gestures for us to go with him and we all follow the direction of the shout.

Three of the Rads are gathered around bodies on the ground. One is Virge. He's lying at a strange angle and there's a dark hole in his chest. Next to him is one called Tam. He has two wounds in his side which are still bleeding. Hornet and Livia are trying to staunch the flow.

"Can you see anything inside?" asks Singer. "What got him? Those aren't cannon wounds."

"Shrapnel of some sort," says Hornet without looking up. "Maybe even some of Virge."

That makes me feel ill.

Julius bends down.

"Hey, Tam. How do you feel?"

Tam turns pained eyes on him.

"Hurting, J."

"We'll give you a local. Get out what you can," says Julius. "Then we'll see what else we can do for you."

He stands up.

"Do it fast, then clean it up. The drone will have sent our location to Borealis, or maybe closer units. We need to move quickly. Bury Virge as much as you can. We can't do much more out here."

I don't stay to watch them digging around in Tam's side, so I help with Virge's grave. The ground is quite easy to dig until you run into roots, but we manage a shallow grave. I look away as they place Virge in the hole and can't bring myself to do more than put a couple of shovels of earth on his legs. Once it is done, Livia stands briefly by the fresh earth.

"Here lies Virge," she says. "Blood of earth. We'll drink to you when we can."

A few minutes later, Julius comes along with Double and Stubble.

"Sherman," he says with a smile. "Would you like to come with me please. I'd like some help from your expertise."

Sherman and Lee exchange glances, but Sherman stands up and goes along with them. I can't believe Sherman has fallen for such simple flattery, but then again, maybe I can.

A few minutes later, I hear a shouted "No!"

It is Sherman's voice. Lee is on his feet and so am I, running to see what is happening. Rash, Livia, Singer and another, bar our way. On the other side of them, I can see Sherman is being held down on the ground by Double and Stubble. He is thrashing around, but Double's weight on his chest and Stubble's on his legs are too much for him. Julius is holding his knife and there is a line of blood on the blade. Double has hold of Sherman's right arm and I can see a cut on it. Hornet is helping Tam to sit up while Double moves his arm closer to Tam's mouth.

"Bastards!" says Lee and tries to fight his way through. Rash and Singer go to grab him and he swings his cuffed hands at them. Singer goes down, but Rash is fast and wiry. He jabs at Lee's side under his ribs and Lee crumples. Then Rash is on his back in a flash, pulling his forehead back and putting a knife at his throat. I didn't even see him pull it, he was that fast.

"I'll cut you too if you like, Bluey," he snarls. "Just give me an excuse."

Lee is sweating and breathing heavily through his nose. He reminds me of a bull, but there is nothing he can do with the blade on his jugular.

Livia is eyeballing me too, daring me to make a move. But what can I do? Her eyes are so like Julius': the pupil in a grey-blue iris.

So we have to watch as Tam fixes his mouth on Sherman's arm. We have to watch as he sucks greedily, encouraging the freshly flowing blood. When he is finished, Hornet wipes Sherman's arm across the wounds themselves.

"There," says Hornet. "We'll see where that gets you, Tam."

Double lets go of Sherman's arm and he snatches it back, cradling it to himself and looking at the cut.

"Don't worry, curly," says Hornet. "You'll be fine. And just think, you might have saved Tam's life too."

"Okay," says Julius. "Everyone on their feet. We need to make tracks."

Sherman picks himself up and Rash slips off Lee's back, giving his head an unnecessary push on the way.

"Come on, pretty boy," he says. "Any of those drones come back and I'll use you as a shield."

[11]

I JUST HAVE TIME TO dress the cut Julius made on Sherman's forearm before we set off.

"I don't care if the nanomeds will clean it," he says. "I want you to do it. I don't want any of that filthy Rad's spittle on me."

He's angry and shaken and lapses into an unusual brooding silence once we start walking.

There's an urgency to our movement now, as the reality of pursuit has become more real. That's not to say we're moving quickly though. Tam is slowing us down. Lee is also claiming his shoulder is hurting and complaining about the pack he has to carry, but Julius doesn't believe a word of it. Neither do I.

We reach a stream and follow it uphill. When I catch a glimpse of the mountains, I see we've changed direction to be south of where we were tracking before.

We have to stop often for Tam. The contents of the packs he and Virge were carrying have been split among the rest of us and it more than makes up for the food we've eaten over the last few days. Double is carrying both the boomer and one of the other rifles now. He must be very strong because I picked up one of those rifles when we were at the copter and I know how heavy they are.

Julius, Singer and Livia confer every time we stop, huddling over a tab. They are very animated, but I don't know what they're talking about.

We're just stopping to pull lunch out of our packs to eat on the move when Singer raises his hand. It's already come to be an ominous movement.

"We've got a copter," he says, his eyes nervous behind his glasses.

"How many?" asks Julius.

"Just one, but it must be a carrier. They're back where the drone found us."

There's immediately another huddle. Afterwards, we cut away from the stream, so maybe they've been arguing about which way to go.

Then Tam collapses.

We all stop. Julius looks troubled.

"I'll carry him," says Double.

"You can't," says Julius.

"I'll leave the boomer."

"We'll need that."

There's a pause and the unit exchanges glances.

"You're not going to leave him behind?" says Hornet.

"What other choice is there?" asks Julius. "We're going too slowly. If they catch us out here, we're all dead anyway."

"We could milk the Blue again," says Rash.

Hornet shakes his head.

"There's no point. He needs time for the nanos to get there and do something."

"And we don't have that time," says Livia.

She's watching Julius.

Everyone knows she's right, but no one likes it.

Julius pushes his hand through his hair, then he looks down at Tam's grimy face.

"Leave me a gun," says Tam. He's opened his eyes. "J's right. Leave me a gun. I'll take some out for you."

No one says anything for a few moments, then Rash takes the assault rifle from Double and places it in Tam's hands.

"Make sure you save one for yourself," he says.

Hornet grips Tam's hand. You'd think someone called Hornet would be some kind of tough guy, but he seems the gentlest of all of them apart from maybe Singer. Maybe it's just the glasses, but Singer seems the smartest of all of them too.

Glasses. I've never thought about that before. You don't get blue-bloods wearing glasses because the nanomeds fix their eyes.

Everyone shakes hands with Tam. Everyone but the three of us. They've propped him up against a tree stump with foliage around him. You'd have to walk right up to him to find him. I wonder how he feels to be left alone in the woods.

We immediately make better progress. We're still moving up hill. My pack is heavy. Most of the weight is in the ammunition. I don't suppose I'd be able to persuade Julius to let me dump some of it. At least we didn't take all of Tam's with us.

Abruptly the forest opens up into a large clear area. Inside it there is an L-shaped group of buildings made of steel and concrete. Next to them are half a dozen silos. There are railings on the top of each one and they are linked by narrow footbridges.

Julius turns around to face us.

"Brag, Singer – it's time to lighten some packs. Double, Hornet, Livia, Stubble – set up a perimeter. Rash, Eames, with me."

[12]

WE FOLLOW JULIUS OUT INTO the clearing. It's not a true clearing, but most of the trees in here are no more than saplings. We pass overgrown piles of timber and I can see now that it's an old sawmill. Over to one side, I see a road going out. That's half grown over too.

Julius seems to know where he's going. He heads for the largest building. There's a faded red door, paint peeling. It opens and we go inside. It's dark and smells of damp and old wood.

He switches on the flashlight under his rifle barrel and uses it to guide us. The room is full of old machines, some reaching up to the concrete ceiling. There are stretches of concrete wall and steel pillars at regular intervals holding it up. There must be heavy machinery up there too. Down here are a couple of conveyor belts running the length of the room. One goes out through an opening in the far wall, letting in a little light on that side.

We cross the room. Julius stops at a standalone piece of equipment that looks like a bench and drill combined. It turns out to be on wheels as he pushes it and it moves over to reveal a square metal trapdoor lid set into the concrete floor. He bends down and opens it to reveal a ladder.

Julius goes first to light the way, then one by one we all go down. The space is lined with brick and empty apart from a small chest of drawers against a wall, a wooden chair lying on its side and a couple of cardboard boxes. I was expecting it to be damp, but it's not. The floor its gritty, but otherwise clean.

Julius checks the brothers' cuffs, then sits them in opposite corners of the room. He puts me in a third corner, but I'm not cuffed. Eames goes to the drawers and takes out a couple of candles which he lights by pulling a splinter of wood across a small box. This makes a flame which he touches to the candles. The gentle light fills the room and makes it feel like a more welcoming space.

"What's happening? Why are we down here?" I ask.

I feel like I'm asking it for the boys too, but I can see they're being taciturn hard men and think asking questions will show them as being weak. I don't care about that; I just want to know.

"Keeping you out of the way," says Julius. "Some of your friends will be here before too long and it would be a shame if they put a bullet in one of their own."

"You should surrender now," says Lee. "If that was a carrier it'll have forty men on board. They'll be fresh and highly trained. You're heavily outnumbered and outgunned."

"I know," says Julius and winks at him. "It's gonna be fun."

Then he goes up, leaving Rash and Eames with us.

"Well he seems confident," says Sherman. "How about you two surrender to us now and at least you won't get killed."

"Quiet," growls Rash.

We all sit there in silence in the cellar. There's nothing much to do except glance at each other's faces and look at the two candle flames bucking in a draught from somewhere.

Sherman is looking lively and inspecting the room and its occupants. When he catches my eye, he grins, but it's not the usual Sherman smile. There's a tightness about the corners of his mouth. Lee is lost in thought and staring at the floor. From time to time his shoulders move. It takes me a few moments to guess he's testing out the cuffs and probably trying to get out of them.

Eames is leaning back on the wall, his rifle across his legs. He's lanky with a thin face and his black skin glows like silk in the candlelight. Rash is pacing. He's like a scowling, caged tiger, clearly frustrated at being down here with us.

Suddenly he makes for Lee, grabs him by the shoulders and spins him round so that he's facing the corner.

"Now I can see your cuffs, Bluey," he says.

He's sharp-eyed. With all that pacing, I hadn't thought he was paying any attention to us. He's also stronger than his wiry frame would have you believe. He must be all muscle. His pacing continues and the rest of us return to what we were doing, except now Lee is still. And angry.

I jump when the trapdoor opens. Rash and Eames jerk their rifles up, but quickly relax. It's Julius, but his face looks like thunder.

"Eames," he says. "We need you."

"What's up?"

"The remotes aren't working. I need you to sort them out."

"Has Singer taken a look?"

"Yes," says Julius. There's exasperation in his voice, but I also hear a note of fear.

"Then what difference am I gonna make?"

"I just need you to look. You might see something he hasn't."

Sherman is grinning. Lee has turned his head. He too is listening.

"Having some trouble?" Sherman asks.

Julius frowns at them, then beckons Eames up the ladder. They both go up top and keep talking. We can still hear them, because they've raised their voices.

"We're severely limited if we can't get these working," says Julius.

"And the batteries are good?"

"Yes. That was the first thing we looked at."

"And the connections?"

"Of course we checked those!" Julius is angry now.

"I'm sorry J, that's all I know."

There's silence from up top for a few moments. Then Julius speaks again. More quietly this time.

"Okay. We've got to move out."

Julius comes down.

"What about sight lines?" I ask.

Julius rounds on me, his face angry.

"Have you checked the sight lines between the remote and the devices?" I say. I don't know what comms they're worried about, but it sounds like an easy problem to solve.

His face softens, but Lee has tensed and Sherman is frowning now.

"If you have something blocking the line of sight between the remote and the devices then the signal might not get through it."

"What sort of things?"

"Depends," I say.

"Come with me." He holds out his hand.

[13]

SHERMAN IS LOOKING AT ME in shock. To be honest, I'm surprised at myself, but it's just what I've always done. If I hear about a problem that I can help with, then I've always tried to lend a hand. It's how I've learned. Maybe it's how I've survived too. If I'd just sat around fetching and carrying things like most of the domestics I know, I would have gone out of my mind.

So I ignore the obvious disapproval from my employers and follow Julius up the ladder and into the gloom of the large room with the machines.

"Where did you learn about comms?" he asks.

"Here and there. I'm just curious about stuff and one thing led to another."

I'm reluctant to let on how I've dabbled in the military grade gear that the Colonel has at the house. It was patched into elements of the home equipment, but otherwise used a different network. The Colonel didn't always close it down fully, so I could go in and have a bit of a poke around when no one was looking.

"Well, see what you can do," says Julius. "We've rigged up some rifles on top of the silos and some explosives to go off once we've lured the Blues in."

I hesitate. So that's what they're for. Is this something I should get involved in? This is about weapons. This is about killing people.

"Mouse, are you still with me? We don't have all day. We need to get out now if we can't fix this. Take our chances in the trees, but I don't think much of them."

I look at Julius. His eyes are on me. I'm not sure how long I was quiet just then. I feel flustered. There's no time to think.

"So where's your remote?" I ask him.

He leads me over to the back of the big room we're in and we find Singer with his tab running through half the settings.

"Where's Brag?" Julius asks.

"He's joined the others on the line," says Singer not looking up.

I look around the room. He's crouching right behind a large steel hopper full of chunks of wood and sawdust and on top of the concrete reinforced wall, the far side has been lined with girders, sheet metal and concrete to strengthen it so that it can carry the industrial elevator. I point all this out and Singer rolls his eyes and looks irritated. For a moment, I think he's annoyed with me.

"Damn, sorry J. I've been so focused on the gear I forgot to look around me. She's right. The signal won't get through all that, especially not when we're splitting it so many times. Really we should have hooked them up to several tabs."

"Yeah, but we've just got the one. Come on, let's find a better place to sit."

The three of us go out into the open space between the L-shape of the buildings and the crowd of silos. It's deserted and I can't hear anything.

"Where are the others?" I ask.

"Around," says Julius.

"I've got connection with the silo tops already," says Singer. He's still irritated with himself.

There is a sound of distant gunfire. Singer and Julius freeze.

"They've reached Tam," Julius says quietly.

There is a moment. We're all thinking of Tam alone in the woods with the troopers closing in on him. There's an explosion.

"Come on," says Julius. "He's buying us time. Let's use it."

Suddenly I feel like I've got a real reason for doing this. It's to protect me. Those soldiers won't know that I'm here and they wouldn't care if they did. What I don't know is whether they know Sherman and Lee are with us.

"I'm getting signal from the explosives now," says Singer. "But it's no use out here in the open." He turns to me. "We need to find somewhere that's under cover, has escape routes and sight lines."

"You don't ask much," says Julius. "Forget the escape routes. I'll take the tab if we need to."

"Let's try for all three first." I say.

I don't want Julius to be killed. Singer leads us up steps that spiral around the outside of one of the silos. We move between them via the bridges that connect them all on a winding track.

On top of two of them, assault rifles have been set up on gimbals that enable them to be swiveled and tilted. There's a good view from up here. The highest silo is actually taller than the surrounding trees. The gunfire has been continuing sporadically since we came up from the ground, but then it stops abruptly. We all exchange glances. We know what's happened.

Suddenly there's an explosion.

"What was that?" I ask slowly.

"He took some with him," says Singer.

I try to remember Tam. I didn't know him at all really, but suddenly I get a clear sense of him lying there in the damp of the trees. He must have been lying there waiting for the government soldiers to come to him before using a hand grenade or whatever it was. I wondered what it must be like, waiting for death like that, knowing that death was in your own hands.

"Mouse!"

Julius' voice brings me back to the here and now and I feel very exposed on the top of that silo. There are soldiers out there in the trees and soon they'll be here. I take a deep breath and try to focus.

"Do you have any extension cables or splitter remotes?" I ask.

Singer narrows his eyes.

"To jump the signal?"

"Yeah, something that'll hang between the device and the remote. If you can avoid one or two layers of concrete and steel, you should still be able to get a connection."

"I should have a couple in my pack and there might be others here in the cache."

"Great." I look at his back. "Where's your pack?"

"Back down where I was."

Julius rolls his eyes.

"Get it!"

Singer didn't need to be asked. He's already on his feet and running along the top of the nearest two silos to the steps.

I'm left with just Julius. I look at the gun.

"What's that for then?"

"It'll make them think there are more of us than there are and that we're in places that we're not. This place has got a great view of the surroundings, but there's no easy way out from here. If we put anyone up here, they'd be trapped or an easy target if the troopers have got a boomer, which I'm sure they will have."

"So what's everyone else going to do?"

"Keep moving around. No one stays in one position for long."

We look out at the forest. It had looked so peaceful before, but now it seems threatening. I keep expecting bullets to start whistling around me at any moment.

"How long will they take to get here?"

"About the same as we took. Quicker if they realize we're here or slower if they don't. We've got a little time."

That doesn't help. We watch the trees, waiting for Singer to return.

"Why did you help us?" he asks.

I turn back from the forest and meet those eyes of his.

"You needed help. And that's what I do. It's all I do."

"I thought you were going to be one of those redbloods who likes the status quo, who likes not needing to think."

"I don't know if I put that much thought into it. I figure you're the only people between me and the Corps and the Corps is coming to kill me. They don't know me."

"No. And they wouldn't care either."

"What about Sherman and Lee? They won't want to kill them will they?"

"True. They might go easy trying to find them. We'll have to use that opportunity while we have it."

He smiles and reaches out to me, putting his hand on my shoulder.

"Whatever your reason for helping, thanks for doing it. It could make all the difference."

I feel myself blushing, which is ridiculous, so instead I turn away. Where is Singer?

He comes, breathing hard. He thrusts out his hand with a couple of splitter boxes in, cables tied around them.

"Here are the ones from my pack," he says. "I'll see if I can find some more."

He heads back down the steps.

"Cables?" I ask in surprise. "How old are these?"

"We use what we can get," says Julius.

I had expected wireless ones. Quickly, I unravel the cord on the first, but I'm all fingers and thumbs. Julius takes the other one and unwinds it more slowly than I'm trying to, but he's much quicker as a result.

I try to calm down. I hitch the splitter end into the jack on the rifle's remote sensor and dangle the splitter itself over the edge of the silo. Turns out the cable's useful after all as it cuts out some of the obstruction.

"Done," I say. "Where's the next one?"

I stuff the other gear Singer brought up into my pack. Julius leads me across several of the silos to a rifle that's been set up facing out in the other direction. It too is on a mounting that enables it to swivel and to drop its angle of fire. This one's harder to set up because there are two other silos between it and the courtyard, so I'm not surprised they couldn't pick up a signal for it. I walk around the top looking for the best place to put it, leaning over the rail. Suddenly the rail gives way and I cry out as I pitch forward into space.

[14]

THE OLD RAILING HAS SHEARED away from its fittings and my weight has forced it out from the edge of the silo. The only things stopping me from crashing to the ground are the railings which are still connected to the silo. But for how long?

I grip the metal, but my legs are dangling. It's a good job I'm light because the only thing between me and falling is the strength of my arms. I look behind me. The silo is just too far away for my legs. I see Julius running towards me.

"Don't move!" he says.

I'm too frightened to move. Somehow I still have time to think how I'm no longer frightened by the thought of the soldiers, that the here and now is what is frightening. I would have expected that I could hold on for a while. I'm light and I'm quite strong, so I should be able to do this, but I'm not normally hung out over the edge of such a drop. The whole rail bends and I lurch downward and can't stop myself from crying out again.

Julius is at the edge now. He tries to reach out, but I'm too far. So he goes to the railing itself, taking hold of it where it starts to lead out into space. He pulls and I can feel the movement. For a moment I think I'm going down and I take a sharp intake of breath. It's not enough though and I bounce back out to where I was.

"It's not working," I say.

I'm trying to keep my voice calm. Why am I trying to make out this is normal?

He looks around.

"Wait."

Wait? Where's he going?

He dashes back across the silo and unclips the rifle, lifts it up and runs back. I'm looking back over my shoulder trying to see what he's doing, trying to avoid looking down. I know I mustn't look down. Look at Julius, look at Julius.

He pulls down the bipod at the end of the barrel that someone lying down would normally rest it on if it wasn't on the remote swivel mounting. Then he points it at me. For a crazy moment, I think he's going to shoot me, perhaps put me out of my misery. He shifts the weapon in his hands so that he's holding both hands around the stock. I've lifted one of those guns and I know how heavy they are and he's holding it right at the very end. I can see the effort in his face.

Using the rifle, he reaches out further than he can with his arm. He braces his feet on the top of the silo and hooks the bipod over the railing. With the extra reach, he can go further along the rail and closer to me. He gets better leverage that way.

He pulls and his face contorts with the effort. I feel useless now as well as scared. And it wouldn't take much for Julius to slip and go over the side as well.

I'm moving. I'm moving back towards the silo. All I'm looking at now is the edge of the silo and its flaking rusty white paint, but I can hear Julius puffing through his nose and grunting.

"Now!" he manages.

I don't think I'm close enough.

"Now!" he says again, more urgently. He can't hold on any longer.

I push with my arms and flail my legs back. I touch the silo. I've not got a grip. I feel myself teetering. Then there's a clattering as the rifle hits the top of the silo and Julius has grabbed my hand and pulled me towards him. We collapse, me on top of him. He's got his arms around me and we just lie there, breathing hard. I don't know how long we're there. I can just feel his arms around me and hear the thudding of his heart through his jacket. Or is it mine?

I feel his arms relax.

"Okay," he says. "Let's set this up again. And watch where you're leaning."

I look back grimly at the railing which is still protruding over the edge. My legs feel wobbly. I look at the base of the rail and see the bolts were coming loose on the next piece of rail too. Julius saved my life.

"Thank you," I say.

I can't think of anything else. Telling him that he just saved my life is too much to say.

"I need you to finish the job," he says. Then he grins.

Suddenly I'm giggling like an idiot, except he joins in and we're both up there laughing as if the funniest thing just happened to us. He stands up, fixes the rifle back onto its swivel and tries to connect it to the remote device. I recover my composure and go back to scouting out a good location for it.

I keep well away from the edge, but then it occurs to me that the airborne railing has now answered my problem. Together, we pull it back towards the silo, hook the splitter onto it and let it ping back out where it will now be able to see past the two other silos.

We've just reached the ground again when Singer jogs out of the main buildings clutching a bulging canvas bag.

"I found more. And I even found a remote monitor."

"What's that?" I ask.

"It enables you to see what the remote rifle's pointing at. The tab can do it too, but this old monitor means we have two of them."

We race around the site and one by one they show me two more remote machine guns and then explosives. Some are set inside silos, others in structural parts of the buildings.

"Were we carrying all this?" I ask, thinking there must have been more in our backpacks than I thought.

"Most was already here," says Julius. "We stash gear all over the place you know, not just the things from your copter."

There's a mix of splitters and other gear in the bag Singer found. Some of it is military grade, the rest is possibly commercial grade, but I don't recognize it. I'm no expert of course. I just know what I know. But I'm good at working things out for myself and there are enough splitters for most of the explosives. We're able to move the rest of them.

When we're done, I feel a great sense of teamwork and shared purpose. Somehow I expected Singer to look down on me or be angry with me for showing him up, but he just treated me as an equal and worked with me. That's a first. And I can't pretend I'm not enjoying Julius' respect. He shakes my hand.

"Nice work, Mouse," he says.

Then his perco, his personal comm unit, comes to life.

"J," says a voice on it. It's Livia. Her voice is low, hushed. "They're here."

"Roger that," says Julius.

My stomach drops all over again. I'd actually forgotten why we were doing all this while I was engrossed in the task. Now they're here and I don't know what to do.

"Singer," says Julius. "Give me the tab, you take the monitor. I'll take a separate position in case one of us gets hit."

"What about me?" I ask.

Julius smiles.

"It'll be safer in the cellar. Or you can stay up here with me. We'll all be heading for the cellar soon anyway."

"Why?"

He grins and taps his nose.

"Last surprise," he says.

"So I'll stay up here with you then," I say, trying to make it sound nonchalant. To be honest, as much as I like his company, I've grown to trust him and I think I'll be as safe with him as with any of the others.

"Come on then. We'll take that concrete end of the main building."

Even as he says it, gunfire kicks off from several places on our perimeter. It's returned immediately.

"Hear that?" says Julius as we scamper across the open yard, bent over. "The ones using all the bullets are the troopers. They reckon resupply is easy."

It's true. Even I can tell who is firing. The slow measured shots are the Rads, the returning hail of fire is from the government troops.

[15]

WE ARE INSIDE THE BUILDING now and we huddle up against a wall. Julius gets the tab out. Each remote rifle has a camera on it. It's a great way to see what's going on outside, except there's nothing to see. There are the trees and the scrubby ground around the sawmill, but we can only tell something is happening from the sounds of gunfire.

Suddenly there's movement in one sector, a shape in the bushes. I don't know who it is, but there's someone moving towards the sawmill.

"It's one of ours," says Julius. "Brag, I think from the way he's wiggling."

Then we see another shape. It's crawling through the scrub.

"That one's not ours," says Julius, he's already realigning the gun's scope.

"How do you know?"

"Brag's crawling backwards, this guy's going forwards. You got him Sing?"

"Yep," says Singer through the perco.

The rifle fires twice. The soldier jerks and stops. Brag keeps going.

"Okay, Sing. I'll take north and west."

"Got it," says Singer.

Julius flips the tab so he's only watching two rifles. There's more firing, then it stops. We watch for signs of something. An explosion creates a brief fiery light under the trees and branches are torn off. Smoke rises.

We wait a few beats.

"Guys?" Julius mutters into his perco.

"Okay," I hear Double growl.

"Me too," says another voice I don't know, but Julius recognizes who it is.

"They were after me," says Livia. "I'd already moved."

"Be careful," he says.

"Always," comes the reply.

"She is your sister isn't she?" I ask.

He nods.

"That must be hard."

"What?"

"Sending her out like that."

"If I didn't, she'd go anyway. She never was good on discipline."

There's more firing and things seem to be hotting up. We see two more backing through the scrub. We see more troopers coming out of the trees as well. Julius gets one, maybe two, but he misses the others as they duck back under the trees.

There's a bang and a crash. One camera shows a blur of grey sky, then goes blank.

"They're onto me. The others won't last long now."

"Guys, we can't cover you much longer," he says.

There are more explosions outside. Julius crawls to the door to take a look.

"They've taken the tops off two more silos. They're going after more remote weapons, but they've got the wrong silos so far."

We still have three cameras. There's nothing to see from the forest: the troopers are staying under cover, but there are only four Rads backing towards the sawmill. Then there's another crash, and another dead camera.

"Singer. We got one left each. Hold fire. Make 'em think they got them all."

There's no movement from either side. All the Rads are out of sight now, so we're just looking at the edge of the trees and the scrub. We wait. I'm breathing short and shallow and try to slow it down and deepen my breaths to calm myself.

"Come on," Julius mutters at the tab. "Come on."

More waiting.

"Yes!" says Julius in a whisper.

"Where?" I can't see anything."

"Just a little something. They're using the cover better. I can't get a bead on him anyway. Blue north west 100 yards," he says to whoever is on that area.

"Roger," says Double's voice.

"Half way now," says Julius.

"I got one too." It's Singer.

"Let 'em come," says Julius. "There's probably more."

There's a whoosh and a bang. I hear Singer curse. Julius tries flicking over to Singer's camera, but it's gone too. We're down to one. I feel like I'm about to go blind. I feel trapped. Clearly they're closing in from all sides. And if they've got boomers, there's not much we're going to be able to hide behind.

There's firing from behind us. It's nothing we can see through our camera.

"Brag? That you?" Julius is looking up expectantly, waiting for a response. "Brag?"

There's no reply. He heaves a breath. I want to ask what the silence means, but if Brag's perco's gone, chances are he must be too.

Another whoosh and bang and we see smoke on the side of our image.

"Got some," says Double. "Last dart though."

"Come inside everyone."

An explosion tears through upstairs and shakes the building.

"We're not up there," says Julius quietly. "But we could have been." He turns to me. "I think we're lucky your boys are with us or they would have hit us from the air."

I shudder to think what that would have been like.

A gun goes off, once, twice.

"Sonofabitch!" comes through the perco.

"Stubble, you okay?"

"Just."

A few seconds.

"Sonofabitch! Sonofabitch!"

Each exclamation coincides with gunfire.

Then both stop.

Julius rubs his face.

"I said everyone inside. Now!" says Julius. A frown has set across his eyes, but it's determined.

"What now?" I ask.

"Time to go down."

Keeping low, we head across the room and around the corner, dodging among the machines. We pause at the trap door.

"Time to scoot," says Julius.

The first one we see is Singer who's been inside the whole time. Then there's Double and Livia. And that's all. It's Hornet who's missing. I didn't see him come back from the perimeter.

Double is the last one down the ladder. He heaves the trolley over the trap before sliding the lid back on. He stays up the ladder, peering through a crack of the trap.

I see Eames and Rash looking at the faces that came down, quietly noting the ones that aren't there.

"And then there were six," says Sherman.

Julius shoots him a look. "We're not done."

"You're surrounded," says Lee. "Give in now while there are still some of you left. If it wasn't for us, they'd have levelled this place. We'll make sure you get treated well."

"Oh that's terribly kind of you, second lieutenant," says Julius with mock politeness. "I'm sure the word of a junior officer will carry a lot of weight."

"Tell him," says Sherman.

Lee's eyes meet his brother's.

"What?" says Rash.

"We know the commander of Borealis Base," says Lee.

Rash squints at Lee then marches over to him, grabs him by the collar with his right hand and wrenches at Lee's dog tags with the other.

"Hammond," he says, then turns to Julius.

"So you know Colonel Hammond?" Julius says with a knowing smile.

Lee looks surprised for a moment.

"Oh yes, we know the name of the commander. Related are we? How nice. Well that certainly explains the lack of air support."

"Let me negotiate," says Lee.

"If you're so sure of victory, why do you want to let us out of here?"

"Prizes for Daddy," sneers Rash. He's still got hold of Lee's collar. He flings him backwards. "Not this time."

"Easy with our guest, Rash. Open the tunnel."

What does he mean? My answer comes immediately as Rash, and Eames start to dismantle the wall at the end. They start three feet above the floor and place the bricks down carefully. To my surprise, they come away easily and there is a space behind them.

"Grenade!" says Double who is still keeping watch up the ladder. He ducks and the trap closes above him. Not one, but four or five explosions follow. Then there is a seemingly endless volley of machine gun fire.

"Good job we're down here," says Singer.

But we're trapped down here. Why are the Rads so cheerful? Do they mean to go down fighting? Have they resigned themselves to their fate? Because I'm not resigned to it.

"Julius, what - "

Julius puts his finger to his lips to silence me and nods his head at Double. Double slowly, quietly, lifts the trapdoor lid, then beckons to Julius. Julius climbs up next to him, takes the lid and Double descends. Julius peers around on all sides. Then he lowers it, looks at Singer and nods.

"They're in. Not all of them, but a fair few. It's probably as good as we're going to get. Grab your packs everyone and get out of here."

All of us are ushered through the tunnel opening. Lee resists. Rash pulls his knife out.

"Makes no difference to me, Blueboy. We'll go a lot faster without you. Just give me a reason to bleed you. I could drink a bit in case I need it later."

Lee tries to stare him down. Rash has the eyes of a killer. In the end, it's Julius that ends it.

"Rash, get them through. We don't have all day."

When it's my turn, I crawl through and we're in a damp, root-lined passage. In places there are wooden supports holding up the roof. I think we're all through, but Singer and Julius are still behind us in the basement.

"Mouse!" calls Julius in loud whisper.

I go back.

"Will the remote signal get through that wall?"

Suddenly I'm an expert in comms. How did that happen?

"I think your main worry is the thickness of the floor. It's reinforced concrete isn't it, so it'll be thick with steel to take the weight of all that machinery up there."

"So the wall could be the last straw?"

"This wall won't make much difference compared to what's above us," I say. "The trapdoor is the weakest point."

"Okay," says Julius. "Fill in the tunnel wall and leave just enough to let me through. I'll set it off up the ladder."

What does he mean set it off? Are there more explosives? We start to replace some of the bricks. They have numbers on the tunnel side which must identify where they fit.

"Get down the tunnel," says Julius. "Hurry!"

I do as he says. I haven't gone far when there is a series of explosions. While they're somewhat muffled by the ground, the effect is magnified by the shaking. Chunks of earth fall out of the roof. Ahead of me I can just see the dim light of a torch with a shuffling silhouette behind it that shows the tunnel is running straight. Then the light goes out and I stop, confused. Has something happened? A light shines behind me and I see the tunnel has curved. I keep going.

My knees land on hard objects, stones or roots, I don't know, I'm just crawling. I've never crawled so far. I'm breathing hard. Where are we going? How long will this go on? What happened back there?

I feel a cold draft from ahead. I go on. I don't notice at first because of the torch behind me, but the tunnel has become lighter. It becomes more noticeable and then the end of the tunnel is in sight. Hands pull me out and even the dim light of the forest is bright.

There's no time to rest. As soon as Singer and Julius are out, we're all walking at speed up a wooded slope. Before I know it, I'm sweating under my backpack.

Double is in the lead and he stops at the top of the hill and looks back the way we've come. We all follow his gaze. Through a break in the trees, we can see the sawmill about half a mile away. Or what's left of it.

Large parts of several walls of the main building have come down and all of the silos' tops have been blown off. Some of them are twisted and sagging. Smoke and dust is still flowing away from it. There are troopers moving in and out of the dust. We see several of them moving away from the sawmill, so some of them survived the explosions.

"Come on. That's bought us a little time," says Julius and we're off again.

A thought occurs to me. It's seeing the men in the smoke that does it. Those men were caught in an explosion that I helped cause by helping them fix up their remotes. Does that mean I have taken lives? I feel strange. But they would have killed me, wouldn't they? Or were they my rescuers?

I glance at the brothers. They are neither friends nor family. Although my relationship with Sherman at least is familiar, he is the one who calls the shots on it. I am not relaxed around him because he can decide what happens to me. These Rads though, they are my equals. They're like the friends I have: redbloods. That is why I did it. It was like being vagrant again with the cops after us. Since that time, I haven't felt more in common with other redbloods than I do now.

It's only about fifteen minutes later that we hear the unmistakable sound of a fighter craft. We see it overhead. A dark shape drops away from it, but I lose it as it falls. It's followed by three loud explosions hard on each other. There are a few seconds of sound and fury. The space behind the trees where the sawmill is erupts into fire and smoke.

"Still think you're special?" says Rash to Lee and Sherman.

The brothers exchange a look. Both of them are shocked.

"He must think we're dead," says Sherman.

"Yes," says Lee after a moment. "That'll be it."

"Think what you like, soldier boy, but he'll sure think you're dead now," says Julius. "But they'll still go in and check, so we'd better make the most of our head start."

We trek for what is left of that day and even try walking through the night, but it is too hard in the forest. People keep tripping over trees or getting low branches in their faces. So we camp in a hollow, eating out of self-heating pouches from the copter supplies. I'm ravenous. I haven't eaten since the morning.

It has all been a terrifying experience. Even now, I am scared. They still might come after us. But I am also exhilarated. I look around at the Rads who fought: Julius, Livia, Double, Singer. I feel a strange empathy with them. I helped them fight off those troopers. I was the one to fix their sight line problem. Without me, perhaps everyone would be dead or captured. Or maybe the Rads would be dead and the brothers and I would be on our way to the comfort and safety of Borealis Base. The old confusion resurfaces. Sherman doesn't help. He sits next to me while we're eating.

"What did you do for them?" he asks me, his voice low.

"What do you mean?" I ask.

I'm stalling for time because I don't know how to answer him.

"You helped them with something."

"Oh, they were just having problems with their comms."

He looks at me. I turn back to my dinner. Sherman's not the smartest guy, but he's also not the dumbest either. He could still tell if I was holding something back.

"These guys are serious terrorists, you know that right?" he says. "I don't know how many troopers they took out back there, but father will be furious. If he thinks anyone survived, he'll come after us. I want to know we can count on you."

"For what?"

Yes, I'm stalling again and even I think it sounds obvious.

"You like that Julius guy don't you?"

I arch an eyebrow at him.

"Are you jealous?"

"Mouse, he's a murderer. And a Rad."

He is jealous.

"He only wants what you've got," I say. "The nanomeds."

Sherman scoffs.

"People like him don't deserve what we've got. His actions prove it."

We both focus on our food pouches, shoveling another couple of spoonfuls into our mouths.

"Lee and I need to know we can count on you," he says.

"For what?"

"They trust you. They kind of trusted you before, but now, after whatever it was you did, they almost treat you like you're one of them. We can use that."

I eat my final mouthful and follow it up with a swig from my canteen.

"I'll keep an eye out," I say.

Once more, it doesn't actually mean anything, but Sherman takes it as agreement. I glance at Lee. He's staring into the trees.

Sherman may think the Rads trust me, but they don't give me a watch during the night. I can't say I mind because it leaves my sleep unbroken. I must have been exhausted because I sleep like the dead and wake, feeling cold, to a dull grey light, the smell of leaf litter and the sound of bag straps and zips.

"Let's get going," says Julius. "No stopping for two hours."

Rash scours the ground before we go. He stoops and picks something up, flashing it at the brothers. It's one of Lee's shoulder pips showing his rank.

"Nice try, Blueboy. It's mine now."

Lee looks away trying to look like he doesn't care, but I can see the anger and frustration in his eyes.

We make good time today. It's amazing how much faster we go when we're not hauling someone injured. Then late afternoon, we hear a drone again. We spread out and keep still. The forest canopy is so thick, we don't even get a glimpse of it, but we still hear it as it flies nearest to us, but still a fair distance away. It only does it the once. There's no way it saw us.

"They know we got away," says Livia.

Julius shrugs.

"We can't keep heading home if they're looking for us," she adds.

"They don't know where we are though," says Singer. "They got lucky finding us before, but the trees are thicker here. It'd be a fluke to find us again."

"They'll use ground trackers," says Rash. "There are nine of us. It'll be easy to follow us on the ground. We're making a path like a freeway."

Julius still doesn't say anything. It's the next morning when we find out what he's thinking.

We have come to the edge of a river so there is a break in the trees which means we can see further ahead than we can when we're amongst them. We must have been walking west because the mountains are right there next to us; steep forested slopes topped by rocky ridges and snowy summits. It would be late summer back in the city, but all this way north, it's much colder and the fall is here.

"We're going over the mountains," he says.

"But the west coast is irradiated," says Singer. "It's a toxic wasteland after the bio-bombs. Only the mountains are holding it back."

"So they won't think we'll go there."

Livia looks troubled and he puts his hand on her shoulder.

"We won't go far in. Just far enough to throw off pursuit."

She doesn't look convinced, but I think she'd follow him anywhere. I think they all would. As for me, well no one really talks about the west coast. It was nuked to death in the war. Not even the east coast got hit so bad, no one except the other side of course. They say half the dirt of Asia was blown into the sky and the Asians had the last laugh when it blocked out the sun and brought us, and them, the long winter. The winter that still hasn't completely finished with us.

Since then, even decades later, it's always just been a place you didn't go. There was never a question about it. Except now it seems we're going.

[16]

I'M FILLING MY WATER BOTTLES when Julius crouches down next to me.

"You're not scared of the mountains are you?"

"How safe are they?"

"Look Mouse, I've lived in these woods a long time. You can't live down here without going up there. At least I can't." He waves his hand towards them and his eyes shine. "Look at them. They're beautiful. They used to be a place where people would go to relax. Can you believe it? Now they're a wall to keep out the pollution in the west."

"Have you been up there before?"

"I've been up this side. They're pretty wide you know. And it's not all mountains. There are the high plains." He pauses and looks away but inward at the same time.

"And somewhere, somewhere beyond the mountains, it's got to be different. Somewhere we won't have to keep running from the troopers. Somewhere they'll leave us in peace."

I'm done filling my canteen.

"Taste the water," he says.

I take a swig, watching him as I do.

"What do you think?"

It's cold and good. The water tastes different out here compared to the city. It's the only thing that's been stopping me thinking it's going to kill me with radioactivity.

"Good," I say.

"Yeah! It's mountain water. It's snowmelt. It's naturally filtered through the rocks and the mosses as it comes down to us from up there. I've drunk gallons of it. If it wasn't healthy, I'd have lost all my hair by now or be dead."

He has a point. He has a good head of hair. You could put your fingers through it.

"So, this side at least is good. It's the coast itself that took the beating. If we stay high, we should be safe."

And that's how long it takes to convince me. Maybe I'd follow him anywhere too.

Going uphill is much harder than the up and down of the forest. Julius walks with me and tells me that we're following an old logging road, but it's pretty overgrown.

I'm getting used to my pack and living outdoors. I haven't had a shower for a week, but I don't feel dirty like I did in the city. Here, the grime is just my own sweat and the dirt from the ground. I'm feeling fit too and no one is slowing us down.

Sherman and Lee with their military training were always fit anyway and they've stopped trying to slow us down. That's a battle they've given up on for now.

So up we go, climbing steadily higher until we can see the forest spread out at our feet, reaching away to the central plains further east and the lakes of the northern wilderness.

I take deep breaths of the clear air. It is invigorating. I can see why our ancestors came up here for fun. We might as well be on a different planet compared to the cities.

We're about to leave the forest behind and head up a valley that will take us deeper into the mountains, so we stop to take a last look.

We can see the distant ruins of the sawmill from up here. Julius takes the field glasses and surveys it.

"Not much left of that place," he says. "But it served its purpose."

He continues to scan, then he pauses. He has been looking at one spot for a long time. When he's finished, he lowers them slowly.

"I can't be certain," he says. "But I think I saw someone down there. They're still a long way behind us, but they're looking for us. I was right to come this way."

With that, he turns again and we're walking into the mountains.

You could forget there's a war on up here or that there ever was one. The only sounds are the birdsong, our footfalls on the ground and the swish and snap of breaking through any undergrowth. No one is talking and everyone is lost in their own thoughts. I find I slip into an almost meditative state where I go long periods without any idea of what I might have been thinking about.

Thoughts swim through my head, thoughts of Julius, Sherman and Lee, three completely different kinds of men. And I wonder what is going through the mind of their father, the Colonel. Would he even be upset at their deaths or are they just soldiers to him? Surely he would feel something, although I've never seen him show any affection towards them.

I think of friends in the city and I think of Grandad. I'd love to show him this place. I think he would like it. I think he would approve of the mountains in the same way he dreamed of going to the stars. Perhaps that's why people before the war enjoyed the mountains, because they were reaching for the stars too and it was the only way they could get close to them.

We set up camp for the night, just above a stream, and the sound of running water lulls me to sleep and fills my dreams. I wake in the morning excited at the prospect of exploring deeper into the mountains. Few people have ventured up here for decades.

We pack up and climb higher and higher. We come out above the trees and we're into grass. There are even patches of snow up here, hiding in shady places behind rocks. The clouds have cleared and a wide blue sky is smiling down on us, but we've already lost the sun over the other side of the range. There are peaks visible in the distance, covered in snow. They look so close, but there's nothing near them to provide scale; no trees or bushes or, of course, people.

I'm beginning to find it harder to walk and am starting to get a little breathless more quickly. Singer notices and I'm pleased to see he's puffing a little too.

"It's just the altitude," he says. "Much higher up and it can make you sick. At this height you'll get used to it."

"Good," I say. "I thought I was getting old!"

"Yeah, you're just a little old lady," says Sherman as he goes past. He still looks like he's walking down on the level and I'm jealous of his level of fitness. Lee looks fine too.

I frown to myself. I would have thought the Rads would be used to walking out here. I would have thought that if they were putting in extra effort, then Sherman and Lee would be as well, but they're not. And when I look at Rash, I see him watching the brothers too.

He falls in behind them as they're walking side by side.

"You two are in good shape," he says. "Do a lot of altitude training do you?"

"We do a lot of physical training," says Sherman.

Rash keeps watching them for a while.

"It's the nanotech isn't it?" he says. They don't respond. "It does something." He turns. "Singer, what could it be doing?"

Singer pushes his glasses up his nose.

"Maybe it promotes the production of hemoglobin or something to carry the oxygen."

"Well does it?" says Rash. His tone is threatening.

"If you say so," says Sherman. "I don't know the science, I just carry it around."

Lee, as usual, says nothing.

That is as far as that conversation goes. I suppose it would make sense that their blood does that. If it can respond to injury, I suppose a lack of oxygen because of altitude is equivalent to a kind of injury.

We set up camp next to a small lake. We filter the water before filling our canteens. Singer says it's not about toxins from bio-weapons, it's about what animals might have done in it.

The stars come out and they seem even clearer up here. It's certainly cold. I put on all the layers I have in my pack, but my sleeping bag still isn't warm enough. I huddle down and wait for my body to warm it up. We have small, inflating mats too. They don't provide much cushioning, but they do stop the cold of the ground getting through.

To take my mind off the chill, I look at the stars. In the city, you can only ever see a few because the bright lights drown them out. I'd noticed they were clearer in the forest, but we could only ever see a small patch of sky through the branches. Here, there's none of that. It's breathtaking. I had never thought there could be so many stars, that so many points of light could fill the sky. I make a little square with my fingers and hold it up and start to count the stars inside it. I get to a hundred and lose track of which ones I've counted and which ones I haven't. Across the middle of it, there's a broad line where the stars are more dense. Grandad told me about the Milky Way. He told me that we're looking at our galaxy side on and that we're on the outer edge. Suddenly this world feels very small.

I don't notice that Julius has wormed his way over to me until he speaks.

"What do you think?" he asks.

"It's amazing. There are so many."

"You think these forests are big until you look up. Over the mountains, or out there, there's so much to see. These Blues, they could do so much with their technology. It's evolving all the time. One day it could help us to live out there. I want to be part of that. Don't you?"

"Well I'd like to go out there, although I've heard Mars isn't all that hospitable. Maybe nanomeds would help."

"Oh I bet they could. They're the next step in human evolution."

I can hear his smile in his voice and when I turn my head towards him, I can see his face in the light of the stars, his teeth gleaming in a smile. I can feel the warmth of his breath.

"But it wouldn't be us evolving, would it? No more than it was me flying over the forest when you shot me down."

"Sorry about that." He chuckles. "Still, it worked out okay didn't it?"

"Not for Tam and Stubble and the rest."

"Ah, they took some with them."

We are silent. Maybe he's gone to sleep.

I wake early with the sun. Its golden light reaches us a few minutes before it touches the forest down below. I'm cold again, but I'm enjoying seeing the early light on the mountainside.

Someone walks across the camp, his dark shape silhouetted against the dawn sky. It's Rash. He must be on watch. He bends down near one of the other sleeping bodies and there are muttered voices, but I can't hear what they're saying. Another Red struggles out of his sleeping bag. It's Double. They cross the sleeping camp.

They stop at Sherman. Something is worrying me. This doesn't feel right. I see Rash's knife. For a moment, it catches the light of the sun. Then Double bends and grips Sherman on both sides and Rash is down. Sherman cries out and I know Rash has cut him. I don't know where, but Rash has his head down. I can hear his slurping at Sherman's blood. Sherman is thrashing about, but Double and Rash between them are holding him still.

The whole camp is awake now. Lee is struggling out of his sleeping bag. He's on the other side of the camp from Sherman. They've been separated so they can't talk to each other in the night. Before anyone can stop him, he's launched himself at Rash, pushing him off his brother. Both land sprawling on the ground. Rash kicks Lee off him and is quickly on his feet, crouching, ready to spring. Lee is in the same position, but with his hands together like a club because he's still cuffed.

Julius jumps between them.

"Enough!" he says. "What is going on?"

"Blueboy doesn't like me taking his brother's blood," says Rash.

"Why are you doing it? You're not hurt are you?"

"Call it an experiment," says Rash. "I wondered if I had me some of his blood, whether I could walk without tiring like these guys do."

Julius' posture relaxes and he nods his head slowly.

"Well, that is interesting. Let me know if it works. And next time, don't make such a scene out of it. I thought we were under attack."

I'm disappointed by Julius' response. I wanted him to stop it, not condone it. Instead he turns to Lee.

"Sit down, lieutenant. We're just taking what's been withheld from us by the government. You need to behave in future or we'll tie you to something in the night which will make sleeping even less comfortable for you than it already is."

Lee holds Julius' gaze for just a moment, then slowly walks back to his place. As he does so, he glances in my direction. When he sees me watching, he looks away again. I don't know whether he was brave or stupid, but I'm glad he did that. There's something about this blood-sucking that seems so wrong. Julius makes it all about the technology in the blood, but it's more personal than that.

I go over to see what I can do for Sherman.

"What do you want?" he says. His voice is sullen.

"I was going to see if you needed anything."

"Not from you," he says. "Not unless you can get us out of here. If Julius is right and there are troopers following us, we could be back with them in hours."

"But then you'd come back and kill them all wouldn't you?"

He frowns at me. "Who's side are you on?"

I look down.

"I don't know."

"You'd better decide."

We break camp quickly after that and are soon walking in the crisp, cool air. Rash has an unpleasant smile on his face. His face doesn't suit smiling. He goes up to Sherman.

"I feel good," Rash says. "Maybe it's a good night's sleep or maybe it's your blood giving me a bit of a boost. What do you reckon?"

Sherman ignores him and Rash chuckles and moves ahead.

We're higher by lunchtime and the patches of snow have grown. They are on the slopes around us as we pause to eat.

"How are you feeling?" Julius asks Rash.

"Not as good as I was. I'm pretty sure that blood did something for me though."

Eames cries out and slumps forward at almost the same time as we hear the faint crack of a gunshot. Everyone, including Sherman and Lee, dives onto the ground and scrambles for shelter behind boulders.

"Where did that come from?" Julius hisses. "Rash check on Eames."

"That was long distance," says Singer. "It took a while to hear the gunshot."

Rash wriggles on his elbows over to Eames. He rolls him onto his back. There's a neat, dark hole in the top of his chest.

"He's alive, but he's not going to last."

"Damn," says Julius. "How did those troopers get up here so fast. They can't have used a copter, we would have heard it."

"It's their blood," says Rash, menacingly. He grabs Eames' back-pack from the ground next to where he was sitting and crawls up beside Julius and peers around the other side of the rock. He pushes the pack out into the open and slowly moves it upright. It kicks back in his hand and we hear the sound of the shot again.

"Gotcha," says Rash. "I see him. Or I see where he is."

"Is there just the one?" Julius asks.

"Can't say. There's got to be more than one though. So they won't be expecting us to come after them."

"What makes you think we're going to?" Julius asks.

"Because I'm going after them. You guys get on ahead and I'll catch up."

"That could take too long. I'd rather we didn't split for so long."

"J, you need these bastards off our tail or there will be none of us left to go on. I'm volunteering before you even asked. Just one thing though."

"What?"

"I'll need to milk Blueboy before I go so's I've got an edge."

[17]

LEE PUTS UP A STRUGGLE as they all hold him down. I can't bear to see them do it, yet it also seems to make sense.

"Just think of it as me saving your life," says Rash just before he cuts him. "From that distance, they ain't seeing faces and your uniform's so bush-bashed it could be the same as ours. They'll put a bullet in you and your brother just as easy as they'll put one in me. So, I'm doing it for you."

Lee looks away as Rash sucks at the blood from his neck. I catch his eye for just a moment. I'm surprised by what I think I see in his eyes in that moment. It's shame.

After it's done, we all crawl out of sight. We sit Eames up and make him as comfortable as we can. He's not conscious, but he is still breathing. Just.

Julius stands beside him frowning, but there's sorrow in his eyes.

"You don't have a choice," I say quietly. "We can't move him."

"Yeah, I know. And if we stay with him, we'll all end up like him. Doesn't mean I've got to like the choices I make."

He bends, puts his hand on Eames' shoulder for a moment, then puts his rifle in his hands across his lap.

"Hold 'em off for us for a while, will you?"

He takes a deep breath, turns around and walks away. I follow him to where the others are waiting.

"Seeya later," says Rash. "Save me some dinner."

Then he's off, running up a ridge behind us.

Lee has moved over to Sherman.

"I almost hope he comes back," he says in a voice only Sherman and I can hear. "Then I can kill him myself."

"Okay, let's go," says Julius and we're off, moving as fast as we can.

It's tiring work and it's not helped by wondering if I'm about to get a bullet in my back with each step. We're walking beside a small lake now with a shoulder of hill on our right. When we reach the end of the shoulder, my heart sinks. It had been hiding our next climb.

It looks nearly vertical from here. Across the face of the slope, there is a path cutting backwards and forwards as it climbs. I presume this is an old path from when people came up here more often. At least the top of the path really does appear to be the top. Beyond it is only sky. I wonder if that means that on the other side is the west coast. Despite what Julius said about the toxins, this only adds to my worries.

At the base of the zig-zagging path, I decide not to look up and instead I stare at my feet. Walking in a group helps because you can hear the person coming up behind you and it keeps you moving. At the first turn, I see who's behind me. It's Sherman. He meets my eyes and his look is full of meaning, although I can't decipher it. At the next turn, he gets another chance, saying under his breath.

"Now Rash isn't here, this could be your chance."

He wants me to try to get them to escape. What does he expect me to do? Is he expecting me to come up with a plan? It's going to have to be a good one because I won't want the Rads to know I helped the brothers to escape.

I realize what I've just thought. I've just assumed that if Sherman and Lee escape, I'm not going with them. This really surprises me. Is that really what I've decided? No, I don't think I've decided anything. Then Julius catches my eye. He's walking at the front, a thoughtful look on his face. When he sees me, he grins and raises his eyebrows at me.

There's another question for myself. Do I have feelings for Julius and are they anything to do with why I think I don't want to escape? But what would staying with the Rads bring me? It's a life on the run. When it was just us strolling through the forest and the mountains, it seemed romantic and beautiful, but now we're being pursued by troopers, I'm not so sure. It's back to being vagrant again, only worse, except I like it out here.

I look over my shoulder at the lake. I'm half expecting a squad of soldiers to appear out from behind the hill and start shooting at us.

Deep in thought still, I come back to reality when we reach the top and we pause and look in front of us. Where I had expected to see the west coast and the sea, there are simply more mountains and more snow on their tops.

"You look disappointed," says Julius.

"No, just surprised. I thought this was the top."

He smiles.

"I thought that the first time I came up here. But this is a mountain range, not just a single mountain. I don't know how many mountains there are between here and the coast, but there must be a few or the effects of the bio-weapons and the radiation wouldn't be kept back.

The other thing which sucks of course is that we're now going to have to go down before we reach the next one. There's a valley in front of us with a river running out of the headwall of another valley to our left which contains another lake. I would never have thought there were so many lakes in the mountains, not that I'd given mountains much thought before.

We pause for a snack just over the other side of the ridge, then skid down through scree. The loose stones slide with us and it's fun to slide down along with them.

We cross the stream by jumping between rocks, but there's a place where we just have to get our feet wet. The cold water inside my boots is actually some relief. Then we're across the meadow grass and into some conifer woods.

The light is dimmer and everything feels quieter with just the whisper of our feet on the carpet of pine needles.

On the far side of this, we begin to climb again. I don't think my legs have ever had this sort of work out. Or my lungs. Remembering what Singer said, I watch Sherman and Lee. They really don't seem to be struggling in the same way as the rest of us. Surely it's not just their training. These Rads spend their whole lives tramping about in the wilderness, so they should be at least as fit as troopers, especially one like Lee who hasn't seen any combat duty yet and Sherman who's still a cadet.

There are more mountains at the top of this slope and more valleys. I wonder how wide these mountains are.

"Are we going to wait for Rash?" Livia asks her brother.

"Of course," he says.

"How long for? Do you reckon he's got a chance?"

Julius shrugs.

"As good a chance as any of us. Probably better. It all depends how many of them there are and how much surprise he's able to get."

"How will he know where we are?" I ask.

"He'll know. We're leaving a trail he could follow in the dark. The troopers will be able to follow it as well if they've any sense."

We camp below the ridge behind a makeshift wall of rocks we build to shelter us from the wind which comes up with the sunset.

The next morning, the walking continues. We're going deeper into the mountains and I can only assume that we'll have to turn back and do all this walking again once we feel we've lost our pursuers. Only then, it seems, is Julius prepared to head for what I assume is their base.

It's mid-morning when Livia points out a figure coming down the slope we slept on across the valley. He's alone and moving fast. Julius takes out the field glasses.

"It's Rash!" he says. He sounds surprised.

We wait. It takes a while for him to catch up, but I'm happy for the rest.

When he reaches us, he's panting hard and sweating. He crouches to catch his breath and we all wait to hear his story. Even Sherman and Lee want to know. Maybe them especially.

"So," says Double at last. "Did you get them?"

Rash winks.

"Course I did. There were two of them. It didn't occur to them to watch their back, they were too busy following you guys up. I followed them for a ways, watched them arguing about which way you might have gone, but neither of them was a tracker. Eventually they got to the flat just before the lake. They were on each side of the flat. I snuck around and lay in a gulch waiting for the first one to walk over me, then I got his buddy on the other side with the first one's rifle."

He slips a well-oiled black weapon from over his back.

"I liked it so much, I decided to keep it."

Julius looks puzzled.

"I can't believe there were only two of them."

"There aren't."

"Did you see them?"

"Na," says Rash, shaking his head. "I just asked a few questions. The second boy didn't want to die slow and painful, so he told me a few things."

I don't want to think about what Rash may have offered to do to find his answers.

"You tortured him!" Lee spits.

Rash cocks his head and raises an eyebrow.

"No, Blueboy, I *threatened* to torture him."

"Did you kill him?" Lee says.

Rash gives him one of his looks.

"What do you think I did, Blueboy? Anyways, I found out things that'll help keep us alive. It seems they lost our trail when we reached the mountains, so they split up into groups."

"How many?"

"The boy had some self-respect. He didn't tell me everything. I know there was just the two of them, but from the way he was talking, they weren't too spread apart. I'm guessing, but I reckon they would have heard the gunfire. All I know is they were too far apart for his perco to work. And I don't think they're good up here anyway. Too much in the way."

"You did well to catch up with us."

"I had some help. There sure is some cream in these boys' blood. Before he went, I had me a long drink and for a little while, I thought I'd be able to leap these mountains."

I sneak a glance at Lee and his face is like thunder.

"So we need to get a move on then," said Julius. "You just bought us a little time and maybe more if they lose our trail again." He seems like he's got more to say, but he's looking off into the distance. "I think we've got to keep going west. If they do pick up our trail again, they might be slow to follow it if we're going that way, or not bother at all if they think we're just going to die over there."

"I've been watching radioactivity readings on the tab and so far we're barely above normal," says Singer. "I can't scan for anything else, so hopefully the radiation and the toxins go together."

"Well that's good news. Seems like we've got a bit of time yet." Julius looks around at everyone. "Anyone rather not do it? It's going to be hard walking even if we avoid contamination."

"I'll stay behind if you like," says Sherman. He must be feeling better if he's cracking jokes.

Rash doesn't see the funny side.

"Very funny, but you're going to be a whole lot of use coming with us."

He turns to Julius.

"We should all blood them. I sure as hell noticed a difference with those nanos inside me. My breathing was easier and I had more energy. I don't need any more evidence. Every day we should get a ration of their nanos. It'll keep us going."

Julius seems reluctant or a least unsure as to whether to believe what Rash is saying, but I'm afraid it does make sense to me.

"Why not?" Rash asks. "The troopers have got it. They left all their redbloods back in the trees because they couldn't take the pace. It just starts to even the odds."

"You're right. But we need to go easy. Blooding both of them each day will weaken them."

"Yeah, maybe to our level," Rash snarls.

I hadn't thought about it evening odds. I hadn't really thought about the advantage the troopers have over the Rads in quite the same way. The way Rash talked about it, the nanomeds were another weapon which the government troops have and the Rads do not. Rash wants to use it in just the same way he took the trooper's rifle.

So that is how it happens yet again. This time, Sherman and Lee seem resigned to their fate. Singer makes a cut on each of their arms. I am glad he does it, rather than one of the others. He makes the cut like it is a medical procedure, carefully. Rash just makes a quick slash like it's a knife fight.

The Rads line up to drink the blood. Lee still scowls while they do it. When the Rads have finished, they all look at me, waiting.

"No, I don't think I will," I say.

"You need to," says Livia. "You'll slow us down otherwise."

"Then go on ahead without me. I'll catch up when you camp."

"We're not going to leave you behind."

"I'm sorry. I don't feel comfortable."

"Here," says Lee.

I stare at him. He's holding out his arm.

"These bastards take it from me by force. I'm giving it to you."

He holds my gaze for a moment, then looks away at Sherman. Sherman shrugs and nods his head. Then he holds out his arm too.

"Or you can try some Chateau Sherman. It's a cheeky little vintage."

I smile. It would indeed be easier if I had the nanomeds. I could keep up with everyone in these higher altitudes. It would be strange to take it, but with the brothers offering it to me, it seems so much more civilized. And I have to admit it: I'm curious to see what it is like.

So if I've decided to take the meds, whose will I take? Now they have both offered. I'd rather take Sherman's, but Lee was the first to offer, so really I should take his.

Slowly, I walk forward. I bend down towards his outstretched arm. Singer has already wiped around the wound with an antiseptic cloth and then squeezed it open. This makes the blood ooze out again, delaying the nanomeds having had time to start clotting the blood and sealing up the wound.

I put my lips to the wound. I do it slowly. Unconsciously, my left hand lightly touches his arm to steady myself. I only notice it when I feel the hairs on his skin and the muscles moving underneath as he flinches slightly.

I can taste his blood now. It has that bitter taste that I recognize from my own and there's a kind of metallic taste that I could be imagining. They say that the blood at a wound is loaded with nanomeds because they are attracted to where there's a problem, so maybe I really can taste them.

Someone is squeezing the wound, encouraging the blood flow. I can feel it inside my mouth now, running over my tongue. I swallow and the blood is sliding down my throat. I close my lips around the wound, drawing out the blood with a soft suction. It fills my mouth and my tongue gently strokes the opening in his skin, encouraging more of it.

Then his arm moves away and I bring my head up. I see it is Lee who has been squeezing the wound. I can't bring myself to look at him, but mutter a thank you. It felt very intimate and I feel a blush starting to rise up my cheeks, but no one else is paying any attention except for Singer who is hovering with his antiseptic wipe.

"Right then, if that's everyone, let's get moving," says Julius. It brings me back down to earth abruptly. I've just drunk someone else's blood and now I feel a curious sense of debt to Lee. I put my pack on and we all set off again across the mountains, heading west into who knows what.

[18]

WE WALK ALL THAT DAY. I certainly notice the difference that the nanomeds make to me. I can breathe much more easily. We set a good pace, even uphill, and there's a buoyancy about everyone. The Rads chat and banter among themselves. Lee has gone quiet again after his uncharacteristic behavior and Sherman also looks brooding.

In the late afternoon, I feel I'm getting tired again. The effect of the nanomeds is wearing off as they get flushed out of the body. Now we're getting back to being mere mortals again, or at least most of us are. Sherman and Lee are having an easier time of it of course.

We keep going all afternoon and by dusk we're all flagging. I suspect I'm not the only one hoping we'll stop, even if it's just for a few minutes. I glance at the brothers and they catch my eye.

"Hang on guys, I need a pee," I say to anyone.

As I head for a nearby tree, I see Lee give Sherman a meaningful look.

"Me too," says Sherman.

He heads off on the other side of the trail to where I've gone. Everyone else seems to be taking the opportunity too, finding their own space.

I'm just finishing up when there's a shout from where I left the others back at the track. Then there's another shout and I stand up, my heart pounding. It must be another attack. Lee comes thundering past. Not long after him come Singer and Rash, running hard.

Confused, I return to the track, but there's no one there. Then I catch sight of one of them, Double I think, among the scattered trees which fill this side of the valley over beyond where Sherman went to relieve himself. Then it occurs to me: Sherman and Lee are making a break for it.

I don't want to wait right there on the track on my own. I feel I should follow, but which? It's not a hard decision really. I don't want to follow Rash and Lee and I'd rather follow Sherman and Julius. I jog after them. I feel somehow responsible.

The Rads have split up. I catch up with Double. He's out of breath. The guys were already tired before Sherman made a run for it and Double doesn't look built for running far.

"J and Livia are trying to cut him off, but he's gonna be faster than they are," says Double.

"Which way did they go?"

"Straight up the hill after him."

"Lee ran too," I say.

"Damn. Which way did he go?"

"The other way. Rash and Singer went after him."

Then I hear a shout.

"J!"

It's Livia's voice. She calls again. There's fear in her voice. Then again. More urgently this time. Double and I look at each other and start running towards her voice.

We see her up ahead. She's found Sherman, but strangely, neither of them is looking at the other. They're in the middle of a clearer patch among the trees. Sherman is holding a branch like a club in his right hand and he's looking away into the trees. Livia is doing the same on the other side, but she has her pistol out. She must have left her rifle back at the track. Then I see what they're looking at.

Wolves.

At first I see just three of them, but then I see there are more in the trees. It's a pack and they've half surrounded Sherman and Livia. They are scrawny, wiry creatures. Even from where I'm standing, they look crazed, drooling.

Julius appears, running in at right angles to us. He pauses when he sees the wolves.

"Back away and make noise!" he shouts.

Sherman starts to roar and brandish his stick. Livia starts to shout as well and wave her arms around. I look around me for a weapon of my own. There's a likely looking stick a few feet behind us. I nip back, bend and pick it up without taking my eyes off the scene in front of me.

Julius has raised his rifle to his shoulder and is coming closer. He's ducking his head around, looking for an angle. I think the trees may be in his way.

The wolves aren't looking intimidated by the shouting. Double has unhitched his rifle too.

"Why don't you just shoot them?" I ask him.

"Troopers might hear it."

"Julius doesn't seem bothered."

"He hasn't fired yet."

The animals are closing on Sherman and Livia who are slowly backing away. Their lips are pulled right back from yellow teeth. I can see froth around their jaws. Their fur is patchy and rife with oozing sores. Julius is closer now. He raises his rifle again, aims and fires. A wolf near Livia jumps backwards and collapses, but none of the others seem to care.

"Shoot them!" shouts Julius. "They're getting too close!"

He starts to run around towards us so that the wolves aren't between him and his sister. Double raises his rifle and takes a shot. He doesn't hit anything except maybe a tree behind them. Then one jumps at Sherman. He swings with his stick and the wolf dodges back out of range. Then it starts to run backwards and forwards in front of him. It's trying to distract him while two others try to get behind him. Sherman is struggling to watch all of them.

Another makes a run at Livia. She fires once, then again. The second gets it, but another wolf is onto her while she's still distracted by the one she just shot. It jumps at the arm holding the pistol. She screams and swings her left arm into it, but it's a weak punch from her weaker hand. Two more are on her, before we can react. They both go for her legs, trying to bring her down.

Julius charges in, roaring. Seconds later, Double follows. I don't know what takes hold of me. I should be running away, but I'm not. I go shouting in after them, waving my stick.

The three wolves are pulling Livia down. She's screaming and they're growling and tearing at her. Julius is like a madman. He charges in and from point blank range blasts two of the animals. The third finally lets go and leaps back, only to stand and face him again. Double is there too somewhere. I can't see what's going on, it's just a mass of shouting and gunshots and howling wolves. I'm laying about me with the stick and can hear myself shouting obscenities with each blow. I'm possessed.

Something heavy smashes into me and I'm bowled over and a dark shape flies over the top of me. It's another wolf. Even as I'm lying winded, I'm trying to fight off another one that's on top of me, but it's got hold of my wrists. The wolf that jumped turns and prepares to charge at me again, but a rifle shot throws it backwards and now there's only silence and I'm wrestling with the one on top of me.

It's only then that I hear a voice saying: "Calm down, hold still!"

It's not a wolf on top of me, it's a person.

It's Lee.

I lie still and he picks himself up. Then he puts his cuffed hands in the air and looks behind me. Rash is pointing his gun at Lee. Rash is breathing hard.

"What were you doing?" I ask, pushing myself up from the ground.

"I saw that wolf running for you. There wasn't time to warn you, so I just threw myself at you." I haven't heard him say so much to me for a long time. He's still talking, but this time, to Rash. "Thanks for getting that one," Lee nods his head towards the wolf that jumped over us.

"Didn't do it for you, Blueboy," he says.

I remember Livia. Singer is here too now and he and Julius are kneeling beside her. I run over to see if I can help.

Her clothes are torn and bloody. Her legs and arm have been badly mauled, but she's breathing and conscious. I'm still wearing my back-pack, which no one else is. I whip it off and take out my little medical kit and start to clean her up as best I can, but she's in a bad way.

Singer has taken his tab out. He's holding it over Livia. Then he stands up and waves it over the dead wolves lying around her. He curses.

"J," he says. "It's worse than you think. They're radioactive."

"What?"

"The wolves. They must have come over the mountains from the west. They have a big territory."

"That would explain why they didn't back off," says Double. "I hear there's something about the radiation makes them wilder than usual."

There's a silence laden with meaning I don't understand.

"What's wrong?" I ask.

"If they're from over there, chances are they're toxic too," says Singer quietly. "Their blood, their saliva, damn it, everything about them will be riddled with whatever poison the missiles were loaded with. Look at their sores."

I look around at the bodies. I've never seen wolves before. They're certainly ugly creatures.

Julius bows his head. Then suddenly he's up and grabbing Sherman by the collar and shaking him.

"This is your fault. You led her into them!"

Sherman's surprised by this unexpected assault. He raises his hands in defense.

"I didn't bring us into these mountains! And they would probably have found us all while we were sleeping anyway. We wouldn't have stood a chance."

Double gently takes hold of Julius and Julius relaxes his hold on Sherman. Then he turns to Lee.

"And why did you come back?"

Lee looks away behind him to the direction he had been going.

"I heard her screaming," he says quietly.

"Oh, so chivalrous," says Rash in a mocking tone.

"Thank you," says Julius and my heart is warmed by his generosity.

Lee looks as though he is going to say something, but he bites it back, glances at me and drops his arms.

Julius returns to his sister.

"Let's get her away from these at least," he says. Without a word, Double hands his weapon to Rash and picks her up in his arms like a child. We follow him as he carries her back to the track.

[19]

WE MAKE LIVIA AS COMFORTABLE as we can. Julius made Sherman give her some blood and they rubbed it into her wounds. It will help, but it's clear she's going to need more medical care than we're able to give.

It's nearly dark when the Rads hold a council of war. The three of us sit away from the discussion. We can't hear much of it, but it's animated. While they talk, Julius sits quietly staring at the ground and holds Livia's hand.

We see outspread hands and Julius looking around at the others. His face is dark and mournful at the same time. Then he stands up and walks away from them.

I feel like I should go to him. I stand and walk over, pausing shyly a pace or two behind him. He hears me and turns his head just enough to see who it is before looking away again at the mountains, their tops glowing with the last of the sun.

"They want me to leave her," he says.

I struggle for what to say. What can you say to that?

"They said we did it to Eames. We should do it to her."

"But Eames was as good as dead," I say.

He turns and faces me.

"That's what I said. Eames' wound was fatal. Livia can be saved." He takes a deep breath and his voice has a tremor in it when he next speaks. "She just can't be saved out here."

"I know a place where she can be saved."

The voice is Lee's. I jump because I didn't hear him come up behind me.

"Where?" Julius says quietly. I know where Lee is going to say. I think Julius does too.

"Borealis Base."

I expect fury from Julius. I expect a deluge of words. What I don't expect is another sigh and then silence.

"They'd kill her," he says at last.

"I'd make sure they didn't," says Lee.

"They'd interrogate her. Probably torture her."

"I'd make sure she was treated well."

"You can't."

"The colonel is my father."

"He dropped too many bombs on you to make me think you've got much influence."

There's a moment of hesitation before Lee responds.

"He would have thought we were dead already. And if he didn't, it was the best military decision he could have made."

"And what's my best military decision here, lieutenant?"

"To leave her."

"Yeah," says Julius and turns his back on us again.

"This is a chance of life," says Lee again.

"It's a chance for you to get away," says Julius. "If she's to stand a chance, I need to let you go too."

"So let Sherman go and keep me as a hostage."

"Like I said, your father doesn't seem the kind of man who gives a damn about hostages."

There's not much Lee can say to that one, but the conversation does not feel over. We both watch Julius' back.

"Is death really better than life?" I ask, surprising myself that I have an opinion. "While she's alive, there's hope."

It's so easy to say, but a lot harder to believe. Assuming they did let her live, she could spend her life rotting in a government prison.

"I can't leave her to die," Julius says.

"That's a good decision," says Lee.

Julius whirls on him, his eyes like daggers.

"You don't know what I've decided!"

He strides back towards Livia, back to the remains of his team who are still sitting around her, Singer checking her dressings. Julius gently pushes Singer back and in the same movement he's whipped out his pistol and is holding it to Livia's head. Double and Rash leap to their feet.

"No!" I scream.

Nobody moves.

I can see Julius' back heaving as he breathes. I can't see if Livia is still unconscious, but she makes no sound. The very air is still in the dusk. Sherman is still sitting, looking on with interest. Singer is the closest to Julius, but he's more than an arm's length away. It would be too risky anyway; a nudge could knock Julius' trigger finger.

"J," says Singer very quietly.

Julius is staring at Livia's face. His own face is like a mask, but I can read emotions tumbling from it.

Suddenly he flings the pistol away from him.

I release the breath I've been holding onto.

"I'll go too," he says.

"What?" says Singer.

Julius turns his head and looks straight at Lee.

"Livia will go to Borealis and I will go too. Whatever they might have done to Livia, they can do to me. Save her. Keep her alive. You can have me. I'm of more value than she is."

"No," says Rash. "You can't do that."

"I can't let her die," says Julius.

"And we can't let them interrogate you," Rash says.

"But you three get away. We tell them we're the only ones left. We tell them you don't matter, that you're going to the west and will die there. You three live. Livia lives. I don't care what happens to me."

"Why don't you let Sherman go too?" I say. I can feel the eyes of both brothers on me. "Singer and the others will move much quicker without a prisoner and it'll also be a sign of goodwill."

"And what about you, Mouse?" Julius asks. "Where do you go?"

Where do I go? I genuinely hadn't thought about that. For a moment, I was just outside all of this, forgetting my own stake. I know at once that there's no point in going with Singer, Double and Rash. That would be going away with strangers. That is not the freedom I was thinking about. If Lee and Sherman go, if Julius goes, I will be alone in the world again.

There is only one option.

"Sherman and Lee brought me out here. I go with them."

Sherman smiles. "Actually, it was just me that brought you out here," he says.

[20]

THE GOODBYES ARE QUICK. THERE'S no time for more than a handshake with Julius and a concerned hand on the shoulder for Livia. Rash is eager to be on his way, Double looks awkward and only Singer appears to have something to say.

"Take care of yourselves," he says.

Rash stops and turns around and points his finger at Lee.

"I'll remember you, Blueboy. And you," he adds, looking at Sherman.

"It's mutual," says Sherman. "Been nice knowing you."

Lee says nothing. He just nods.

Then they are walking away into the gloom, trying to put some miles between us and them before they camp for the night. It's only taken a little while. They took some more blood before they went. The brothers seemed almost willing to do it, perhaps because they knew it would be the last time. Then Double, Singer and Rash repacked their packs with most of our remaining rations and ammunition.

So now there are only five of us. It's too late to find any troopers. We wrap up warm.

Some cloud is moving in to cover the stars. I feel lonely. I don't know why.

The morning feels different. It's strange how perspective can change overnight. Yesterday, I thought we were going to be found by the troopers at any moment. Today, I wonder how on earth they're going to be able to find us.

"So do we wait or do we go out and look for them?" Julius asks.

"I think we wait," says Lee. "If we go looking for them, we could get ourselves shot."

"I've got a flare," I say. "I took it out of the copter before we even met Julius. I thought it was a useful thing to have."

"That would certainly make it look like an invitation," says Sherman. "And then we sit out in the open away from any potential cover so they don't think it's a trap."

I hand over my flare to Lee. He has to be the one to fire it. After that, all we need to do is wait for the troopers to arrive. All that time, Julius sits with Livia. He seems to have shrunk. He's no longer a commander, he's just a worried brother.

They come the next morning. First there's a drone. Clearly they're not taking any chances. Next comes the copter circling us. Lee and Sherman remove their uniform jackets and hold them up, assuming someone will be looking at them through field glasses. Finally come the ground troops.

We don't know if it's the unit who have been tracking us into the mountains, but we can only assume it is. They look fit and they look angry. All of us are forced to lie down with our arms spread out. There's a horrible moment when it looks like they're going to shoot Livia because she doesn't comply.

The copter comes down. Livia is strapped to a stretcher and the rest of us are cuffed except for Lee and Sherman.

It's quite a different flight to the one out of the city. I'm suddenly exhausted and with my wrists cuffed, it's hard to get comfortable. Not that these copters are built for comfort anyway. I had room to spread out on the last one, but here I've got a trooper on either side of me. They smell of sweat, well-worn kit and forest. No one speaks for the whole flight, so I'm glad it's less than an hour.

We ride in over the trees and they open up below us to a huge clearing. The forest has been cut down for a wide distance around Borealis Base which is a large rectangle. Down one side is an airstrip, while the rest is filled with buildings in regular rows. As we drop lower onto the copter pad, I can see the base is surrounded by a high concrete wall dotted with watch towers.

We have a welcoming committee. Amongst them is the Colonel who I would recognize anywhere. Two troopers jump out first, but Sherman and Lee are quick to follow. Julius and I are close behind them.

The brothers stand to attention and snap into stiff salutes. Their father walks up to them. He returns the salute. There is nothing that would indicate they know each other, let alone that they are family or that the brothers are back from the dead.

"You took your time getting here," he says. His voice is gruff. I assume this is supposed to be a joke, but Lee doesn't seem to think so.

"Sorry sir. We came as soon as we could."

He walks around them and faces us. He frowns when he sees me. He clearly had no idea I was a part of this at all.

"What are you doing here?" he asks.

"I came with Sherman," I say.

"What's this about, cadet?" he asks.

"Sir, I brought her as my attendant, sir."

"I see. You think you're already an officer."

He looks down at my cuffs and I feel guilty and wonder if he thinks I've fallen in with the Rads. After all, I am a redblood. I can't help but think of the help I gave the Rads at the sawmill. Without me, the place would not have fallen down on the government troops who came inside. I try to neither look away nor look at him in a way that could appear confrontational. I wonder what Sherman and Lee might say about my behavior over the last few days. Now I'm here, I'm beginning to see things differently.

Colonel Hammond has moved on from me. He stands in front of Julius for too many seconds before speaking.

"Well, well. You led us a merry dance didn't you?"

Julius does not respond.

"And now there's just two of you. Or perhaps one."

"Sir, I promised assistance to the wounded girl, sir," says Lee.

"Quiet, lieutenant. Save it for the debrief."

"There are three more out there somewhere, sir," says Sherman.

"Somewhere?"

"We don't know where they went, sir," he says. "They left us when these two decided to turn themselves in."

"I see. They have some head start on us then."

He looks Julius up and down one more time, then walks back around to the front. He puts his hands behind his back and looks at his sons.

"You two, get yourselves cleaned up and report to Field Intelligence for debriefing. And take Muswell with you."

He motions to the squad of troopers behind him and jerks his head towards Julius and Livia. "Take him to the lock-up and her to the infirmary."

A soldier cuts the cuffs off me with clippers and I look up at Julius. His face is somber as he is led away.

[21]

LEE AND SHERMAN ARE SPLIT up. Lee is taken to the officers' quarters while Sherman and I go to a guest facility. Sherman is bunking with a civ contractor whose things are already in the room, although he is not there. Sherman is disappointed. He thought he'd get his own room.

"Get over yourself, cadet," says the sergeant who takes us there. He turns to me. "You're down the corridor at the end on the left. I'm sure you don't need me to show you there."

"Sergeants always get above themselves," says Sherman after he has gone. "Go find the showers."

It clearly hasn't taken us long to get back to the master and servant relationship. If he's feeling sensitive, I'd just as soon not be around him anyway, so I go out to have a look around.

He doesn't have to go far to find any showers because they're just next door, so I go and check out my own quarters. They're much smaller and don't have a window. There is a pair of bunks and beside them, two small lockers, one on top of the other. There is just about enough floor space for two people to stand up. The top bunk looks like it's been occupied because it's unmade.

I set my pack down. There's not a great deal in it, so it should easily fit in the locker. I'm just checking to see which one is empty when I hear someone behind me. I straighten up and turn around. There's a girl standing there in blue fatigues. She looks a little older than me and has her hair tied back.

"Hi," she says. "Find anything interesting in there?"

What I'm doing must look a little odd.

"Sorry, I've been assigned to bunk here, I was just looking to see which locker wasn't being used."

"Bottom one. I hate bending over. Reminds me too much of bowing."

"I can go with that."

"I'm Tinker," she says.

"Mouse," I reply and we shake hands.

"Did you get lost on the way here?" she asks with a raised eyebrow, nodding at my clothes.

I look down. I'd forgotten. I must be a sight. My new clothes that Sherman bought me are torn and covered in a mixture of dust, mud and blood.

"You could say that," I say.

"Well you'd better smarten up, the Colonel doesn't like untidiness."

"I know," I say. Don't I ever?

"Which reminds me," she says going to her bunk. "I'd better make this before the bunk police get here."

She starts to pull at her sheets and blankets with practiced efficiency.

"I normally do it as soon as I get up, but his lordship called from the brig and I had to carry over some hot buttered toast."

She puts on a strange accent to say the second half of the sentence. She seems a little quirky, but I think I like her.

"Who's his lordship?"

"Youngest son of a senator, reduced to logging prisoners in and out of the brig."

"Sounds a bit like mine, except he's still a cadet."

"A cadet? Come up here? What on earth for?"

"He wanted to see some action."

"I doubt they'll let him out of the base if he's just a cadet."

"Too late for that," I say. And I tell her what happened to us. I don't tell her everything, just that we were captured by Rads and chased through the forest and into the mountains. I don't tell her about Julius' magnetism, but I do tell her about him sacrificing his freedom to save his sister.

"I think I saw your man Julius just before. They'd given him a quick session."

My heart skips a beat.

"How was he?"

"Not bad for just after an interrogation," she says. "Tired and pale."

"Had they hurt him?"

"Not physically from what I could tell. But then they always start easy and work up to anything else."

I try not to think of what they could be doing to him or could end up doing to him. It feels so wrong for me to be standing here having a chat to Tinker while Julius is locked up.

"What will they do to him?"

She shrugs. "You probably don't want to know."

Then she looks at me curiously and I wonder how many of my feelings are written on my face.

"What is he like? They say the Rads are like animals."

"What?" I say. "They're just redbloods!"

I think I overreacted. She looks at me slyly.

"And you're a redblood?"

"Of course I am. I'm an attendant." A thought occurs to me. "You're redblood too, aren't you?"

"No, I'm President of the Republic," she says making a face.

"Sorry, just checking."

"This Julius guy. What's he like then?"

I wonder how much I should tell Tinker and decide to play safe.

"He's decent. I told you what he did for his sister."

"Yeah. From the way the officers talk about them, you'd never think that kind of behavior was possible from a redblood. And it doesn't even occur to them that I might be listening or that some of their own men are redbloods."

That is so true. They underestimate us as if the lack of nanomeds affects the way we think. Maybe it does.

"Do they tell you that you're *their* redblood, so that makes it okay?" I ask her.

"They do! I thought it was just me!" She's on fire now. I think I touched a nerve. "God, it's so irritating. Like I got civilized by association. All they've got is robots in their blood!"

I hear Sherman calling me.

"Is that your cadet now?"

"Sherman, yes. I'd better go. He wanted to know where the showers were."

"They should invent a nanomed that can clean them as well."

Chuckling, I leave the room and find Sherman in the corridor.

"Where did you go?"

"Sorry, I was just finding my quarters."

"Oh? And where are they?"

I point to the open door down the corridor behind me.

"Good. Not far when I need you. So where are the showers?"

"You walked right by them. They're just next to your room."

"Right. Find me some new clothes will you? I can't go round in these ones."

I'm not sure where I'm supposed to find some new clothes, so I go back to Tinker.

"If he's officially on base now, the quartermaster will have some for him. I'll show you where it is. You'd better warn your cadet you won't be back in time to towel him off."

"Stop it!" I say with a grin. "He has to report for debriefing in about half an hour. We can't be too long."

“Well that depends on the Q-man.”

The Q-man, or quartermaster, turns out to be a tall, thin, suspicious man who looks down his nose at me when I ask for new fatigues for Sherman. Laboriously he swipes a tab on his desk and flicks through a number of pages.

“Sherman Hammond,” he mutters, then his finger stops as he finds him. “A cadet? I don’t normally have uniforms for a cadet.”

“Then could you just find something that will fit him. He has his cadet flashes.”

“I’d have to think what would be appropriate. Does he have his old uniform at all?”

“He does, but it needs cleaning. Or mending. Or throwing away.”

“Make up your mind.”

I need to control myself. I’m getting too relaxed.

“I’m sorry, sir. We just came back from operations a few minutes ago and I haven’t had time to review his uniform.”

“This is highly irregular. He’d need to fix his cadet flash to any uniform I give you.”

“I’ll do that, sir.”

He seems mollified. He walks into the maze of racks and shelves behind him and is gone for some minutes before returning with a parcel.

“These are his size.”

“Thank you. And do you have some that would fit me, please sir?”

“You? You’re an attendant. You bring your own clothes.”

“I did sir, but they were all destroyed on operation. I’ve only got what I’m wearing.”

I thought that ‘destroyed on operation’ would sound better than ‘lost’. He looks down his nose at me all over again.

“This is highly irregular.”

“I appreciate that, sir. I’m grateful for whatever you can find for me.”

He sighs deeply several times. He looks around as if for inspiration.

"You understand I'm very busy."

"I do, sir. And that's why I'm so grateful that you're helping me. I just thought if anyone would know how to help, it would be you."

He nods.

"I'll see what I can find."

He disappears into the back again and is gone much longer. I start to fidget because I know Sherman will be waiting impatiently. Perhaps I should go and come back once I've dropped off Sherman's uniform, but this may be my only chance to get something to wear.

I'm saved the choice because I see the quartermaster coming back. He hands me some folded clothes. They're blue, like Tinker's, and made of a rough, thick material.

"Base worker blues," he says. "And this is underwear."

"Thank you. That was thoughtful."

He nods again. It *was* thoughtful given I hadn't specifically asked for it. I know base workers are the civilian support workers the military pays to do mundane work on all bases.

I thank him again and race back to my quarters. Sherman is sitting on his bunk in a towel, tapping his feet on the floor with impatience.

"Where have you been?"

"The quartermaster was a bit of a stickler, but I got him to find you something. We'll need to fix your cadet flashes to it."

"Well you can do that later. I've got to report for debriefing."

I leave him to get dressed and take my parcel back to my room. Tinker is on her bunk. I hold up my new clothes in triumph.

"Wow, he ordered something for the little lady too," she says. "Base worker blues! Darling, simply the height of fashion."

[22]

AFTER A FEW DAYS, LIFE has settled into a sort of routine. Lee has dropped in from time to time. He's arranged for Sherman to shadow one of the mission monitors which keeps him off my back. Once I've done his cleaning and made his bed and anything else I can think of, my time is my own. There is little for me to do here. He's simply trying to make himself look more important. At least I've managed to fix up our original clothes. Both came up well after a wash and press and some careful mending.

I hang out with Tinker a lot. She's shown me around the base, as much as she can as there are areas where we, as mere attendants, are not allowed to go. It was clearly put together quickly from pre-fabricated units and heavy duty tents.

The area that interested me most was the brig, the prison unit. Tinker has access to it because she is the brig officer's attendant. She says there are no other Rads in there, that they don't capture many of them.

"Is there any way you could get me in to see Julius?" I ask one day as we're on our way back from breakfast in the workers' mess.

"And why would you want to do that?" she asks me.

"He treated us well. I want to see how he's being treated."

"He's a Rad prisoner. A criminal. They'll look after him well enough that he can still talk to them."

"Is he allowed visitors?"

"I doubt they've even thought about that up here. I suppose they might let you see him."

"I need to be able to bring him news about Livia."

"Who?"

"His sister. They took her to the hospital."

"That'll be much easier to find out. Let's go there now."

We change direction and make for the hospital.

There's a base worker on the front desk and she looks up the record.

"She's in isolation."

"Can we still talk to her?"

"Only with the guard. It'll be through the glass. We can't let you in there unsuited. Contamination risk."

That doesn't sound good.

We follow her directions and find the isolation unit. A guard is sitting in a chair by the glass, flicking through a tab. I can tell by the uniform that she's a redblood soldier. It's much more basic than the blue troopers. That would figure too: this is mundane soldiering work that they wouldn't waste a skilled combat soldier on. She looks up when we enter, a questioning look on her face.

"Hi," I say. "We've come to see her."

"And you are?"

"Muswell. I was with the unit that brought her in. I wanted to see how she was. The wolf attack was pretty gruesome. It could have been any of us."

The guard nods, clearly happy for anything to break the tedium of her shift.

I look through the glass. Livia is lying just beyond it. Her wounds have been patched up, but she is still looking pale.

"How do I talk to her?"

I decided it was better to ask how to do it than asking for permission as that would raise a doubt in the guard's mind about whether I was allowed to.

"Press the green button below the window, there," she says, gesturing.

I press the button.

"Hi. Livia. It's me, Mouse. Can you hear me?"

Livia's eyes flicker open and she moves her head a little towards the glass.

"Can you talk?"

"Yes," she croaks.

"How are you feeling?"

"Weak as hell." She licks her lips. "How's Julius?"

"Alive. I haven't seen him yet. When I do, I want to tell him how you are."

She shakes her head.

"Maybe best not. They say there's nothing they can do for me."

"What do you mean?"

"My whole blood system's contaminated."

"I'm sorry." I don't know what to say beyond that. I've got more questions, but I can't ask her how long they give her. "Is there anything you'd like me to tell Julius?"

She nods, closing her eyes and thinks for a few moments. Or merely gathers her strength.

"Tell him I said thank you for the chance. Tell him I'll hang in there if he does."

I nod. This time, I'm unable to speak. I thank the guard who returns to her tab.

On our way out, we pass a doctor in the ward. On an impulse, I stop.

"Excuse me, sir. I was hoping to update my officer on the state of the Rad prisoner."

"Your officer is?" she asks.

"Lieutenant Hammond, sir. He's the one who brought her in."

"The Colonel's son. Well he won't need to worry about her for much longer. We'll keep her ticking a few more days until the interrogation finishes."

"Okay, thanks," I say before we continue out of the building.

Keep her ticking a few more days? My blood turns cold at the sound of that. Julius only agreed to come in if they kept her alive.

"You've got to find me a way to see Julius," I say to Tinker.

"Why?"

Again, I'm confused about how much to tell her.

"Look, we spent a week together out there. We went through attacks. Yes, we were prisoners, but there were times when we helped each other. He's just a human being. He loves his sister and that's why he's here. I can't just forget about him."

Tinker gives me a long, sly look.

"You mean, he's just a redblood. Like you," she says. I stiffen. "Like me," she adds.

I watch her.

"Do you think it's easy for me to sit in this camp day after day and hear the crap I have to hear about redbloods? Oh, they say they're talking about the Rads, but the Rads are just redbloods with guns. What they're saying, they're saying about me. You want some help seeing this guy who's fighting for me?"

"I do," I say quietly, a little overwhelmed by Tinker's sudden burst of emotion.

"Good, because it's already sorted for you. I told his lordship you'd be bringing Julius something from the brothers, a kind of no hard feelings gift."

"What? Like what?" I say, exasperated.

She shrugs. "I don't know. I figured you'd think of something."

It isn't hard in the end. There's very little you're allowed to give a man in a prison cell beyond food. Fortunately, that is something I am pretty good at preparing, so that's what I take him. I cook up a casserole of canned meat in the tiny galley they make available to attendants over in the officers' block. I take it right over to the brig afterwards. I am in luck because Sherman is at a party in the evening and won't need me or ask where I am.

Tinker takes me over. His lordship, as she calls him, is on duty. Kitson is a second lieutenant like Lee, but the resemblance ends there. He looks a few years older, aided by a thin face and the fact that he actually does stick his nose in the air. I thought that was just an expression.

He lifts the lid on my casserole and sniffs it like he's going to inhale half of it.

"Smells too good to be given to that animal."

"Thank you, sir," I say. "That's why I made you one too." Tinker holds out another tray with an identical covered bowl. "Except yours is a larger portion."

"Take it in. And be quick about it. Follow me."

He rises from his desk and leads us through the complex. He taps the same code into each door we pass. By the third one, I've learned it from watching his fingers. That sure is lazy security.

It turns out that there is another prisoner. He's a redblood trooper who must be on some sort of charge. He's lying back on his bed and ignores us.

Julius is behind bars. He has no privacy from the camera outside his cell. They're outside each cell watching every movement of the inmate. It's just that there are no other inmates. No wonder catching Julius has been such a coup.

He is lying on his bunk when he hears us coming. I can tell he's heard us because he starts into wakefulness. He's afraid. I can tell. He regains control of himself and then looks to see who it is.

"Sorry to wake you," I say.

"Not a problem. I do a lot of sleeping. I can miss some."

He is looking me in the eye. It is more than just looking at me, it is looking into me. He is trying to read in my eyes what is happening, why I have come. I was expecting a smile. No, I was hoping for a smile, but I don't get that. It would be foolish. It would suggest friendship when we are supposed to be on opposite sides.

"I brought you some dinner," I say.

"But they feed me so well in here," he says. "So well, that I always have room for more."

I hold the tray up to a hatch at about waist height and he takes the covered bowl from it. He stays there at the hatch, looking at me.

"It's from Sherman and Lee," I say. "They say no hard feelings."

"That's nice," he says.

"And Livia says to say thank you for trying."

I want to say so much more than that, but I can't. We're being watched by the lieutenant, not to mention the camera. From Julius' face, it seems I've said more than I think I have. His eyes widen at my words. He frowns with a question in his eyes.

"She's riddled with toxins," I add, my voice breaking. "There's nothing they can do."

I hear a chuckle from behind me. It's Kitson. There was me thinking I was going to get told off for saying too much. It seems he doesn't care.

"So you gave yourself up for nothing then," Lieutenant Kitson says.

Julius' eyes move onto the lieutenant for a moment and I see a spark of hate in them, but it fades as quickly as it flared.

"I could help her," he says. He's looking at me as he says it. He's trying to say much more just through his eyes. How can he help her? The medics can't help her; what can he do? That's why we brought her here. And he can't help her while he's in that cell.

"These people could help her!" he exclaims pushing his arms out wide so that the lid falls off the casserole with a clatter. It rolls around on the floor making a noise for an uncomfortable length of time. Julius is looking at nothing now. “They just won’t do it!” he says.

“Time to go,” says Kitson. “Or maybe he wants to eat it off the floor.”

“I’ll come back for the bowl,” I say. “They count pots in the kitchen.”

He jerks his head up to look at me. There’s a light in his eyes again. They’re alive.

“If you want, you can watch the reruns of me eating it. It’s all being recorded,” he says, raising his eyebrows to gesture at the camera behind us. He’s looking at me in that way again. If only I could work out what his meaning was because he’s clearly trying to tell me something.

The lieutenant guides me out to the brig lobby. Tinker is still there.

“Will mine still be hot?” he asks her.

“Yes sir,” she says sweetly. “I’ll lay it out for you.”

I wait for her while she sets a little side table with cutlery, a napkin, a water glass and places the bowl on the table.

“Bon appetit,” she says.

[23]

BACK IN OUR QUARTERS, TINKER goes to sleep, but I lie on my bunk thinking. With Sherman out at the function in the officers' mess, I won't be bothered with jobs for the rest of the evening.

What was Julius trying to say to me? He obviously wants to get out of there, but surely he's not expecting me to help him do that? What can I do?

So that starts me thinking. What could I do to get him out? I think of the security around him. He's in a cell in an army base, monitored by cameras through several security doors and under guard. He's not heavily guarded by people, so that's a plus, but there's still one person on duty at all times. I think I know the security code for the doors. but he's still in a locked cell. And then there's the monitoring camera. Is anyone watching that? Julius made a comment about reruns. Perhaps it's just for reviewing later, if required. Either way, I need to disable it or someone is going to be able to watch me helping him escape.

But even if I'm able to get him out of his cell and out of the prison block, we're still in the middle of an army camp.

A door slams down the corridor. A voice calls out. It's Sherman and he's calling for me. I sigh and throw my legs off the bed and go to see what he wants.

He watches me coming from the doorway to his room. As I get closer, he beckons to me.

"Come on, come on," he says.

When I reach the door, he goes inside and stands in the middle of the room, I see his eyes are slightly unfocused.

"Nice to see you," he says and plants his hand on my shoulder. I can't help giving it a sidelong glance. He doesn't move it. "Now, I just wanted to check that everything is alright with you."

He's trying very hard not to appear drunk.

"Yes, it's all good. I was just going to sleep."

"Oh sorry. Did I disturb you? I'm not sure what the time is. I thought I'd better leave the party early before it broke up anyway. It wouldn't be good form to seem to be hanging around with nothing to do, is it?"

"I'm sure it isn't."

I'm not sure what the purpose of all this is yet. Perhaps just so he can prove to himself that I'm at his beck and call.

"And I needed to check you were okay. After what I heard today, I mean."

"What did you hear today?"

"It's about your friend Julius." He looks at me with meaningful eyes. He still has his hand on my shoulder, so I step to the side to get away from it.

"He's not my friend."

"Of course he isn't."

Sherman doesn't so much smile as leer at me. It's rather unpleasant. But I'm curious to know what he has heard. He must have been talking to a group of junior officers at the party and I'm sure gossip about their one Rad prisoner would travel.

"Then you won't mind what they're going to do to him," he says. He may be drunk, but he's still watching me to see what my reaction is. He may well see a reaction, but I don't know how easily he'd be able to read it in his current state.

"What are they going to do?" I ask, trying to sound nonchalant.

"Pull his fingernails out? Attach electrodes to his testicles? Fill him full of water?"

"They'd do that?" I ask. "Torture him?"

"Actually, I don't know exactly what they'll do to him, but I do know they're going to step things up a notch and start hurting him. He's not being very helpful you see."

"I doubt anyone would be very helpful if they could help it. I mean you wouldn't give in under interrogation would you?"

"Of course not!" he says, waving his hand in a flamboyantly dismissive way. "But would you care if I did?"

I'm getting really puzzled now. I probably look it too. His face goes all serious.

"Because I know you like him. I saw you talking to him and him talking to you."

I don't like where this is going.

"He didn't talk to us like that," he continues. "So it's either because you're a redblood too or it's your pretty face. Which do you think it is?"

"Sherman – "

"I think it's your pretty face. Because you've got a pretty face. There, it's out. I said it. But of course you knew that. I mean of course you knew you have a pretty face, it's your face. But it's out that I think you've got a pretty face."

I really don't like where this is going.

"So, I guess you must be pretty upset about Julius." He sniggers briefly at his little joke. "But I want you to know I'm here for you."

He puts his arms out. I start to back away, but it's hard to get around him to the door.

"Thank you, Sherman," I say.

"You're welcome. I know it must be hard, so I thought what better way to cheer you up than some real blueblood lovin'."

I can't believe this is happening.

He's trying to put his arms around me now. I'm trying to worm away. He's never done this before.

"Because, well, if you put out for a Rad, you must be really desperate for something and I see what it is."

He has both arms around me now and is pushing me back towards the bed. I'm trying to push back on his chest.

"Sherman, no. I'm going now."

"No, don't go. I can look after you. I brought you up here, it's my job to protect you."

I can smell his breath.

"I don't need protecting. Please get off me. I'm going now."

I'm frightened. He's holding me tighter and is bending to kiss my neck. It's disgusting. He's pressing himself against me. I can feel the bed behind my legs. He's pushing at me and we topple over.

"Sherman, please get off me. I don't want this."

"Sherman!"

For a crazy moment, I think it's his voice, talking to himself.

"Sherman!"

"I'm busy, man," he says.

It's Lee. He's in the doorway. He marches over and grabs Sherman by both shoulders and pulls him off. He looks at me with disgust.

"What are you doing?"

"Me?" I'm too surprised to say anything at first. "I wasn't doing anything."

I need to be careful what I say.

"She needed comforting," says Sherman. "She was so upset about what they're gonna do to her friend Julius." He puts an emphasis on the name. "So I was just doing what a good soldier should do to protect the innocent."

"She's a redblood and a servant, Sherman. You don't touch her. You don't see her." He turns to me. "Get out!"

His face is more than stern. He's angry and he looks angry with me which is so unfair. I'm practically spluttering with rage and indignation as I stand up. There's nothing I trust myself to say right now, so I walk out. I leave the room and go down the corridor to my own.

As I walk, I can hear their voices.

"What were you thinking?" says Lee.

"No, what were *you* thinking?" says Sherman, much louder. "She wants me. She's always wanted me. I was just going to make her happy when she's down."

"You don't touch redbloods! You don't touch servants! They're beneath you!"

He hits each word with a hammer and each word is a hammer to my heart. Is that what they think of me? Is that what I am? I've lived with that family for years and I'm a thing that's beneath notice? I always knew that Lee had no time for me, but I didn't realize he thought like that. I'm still shaking from the whole experience, trying not to think about what could have happened.

Then I think about tomorrow. What will I do then? I'll have to face Sherman in the morning. He wasn't so drunk that he's not going to remember it. And even if he was, *I'll* still remember it. I don't know how I'll face him again. Or Lee. Who's to say he's not going to try it again? I'm a nothing; just a redblood civilian in an army base far from home. I don't even have a home, just someone else's house where they've deigned to let me live. I could be gone in seconds. I could be gone tomorrow. Maybe that's it. Maybe they'll kick me out now. Clearly I'm a danger to them and their blue blood.

I close the door and lock it. I want to push something against it, but I know there is nothing. A small light goes on next to Tinker's bunk.

She is sitting on the edge of her bed. Her feet dangling over the edge, her hands pressed behind her as if she were about to spring off.

"Some shouting woke me up," she says. "Was that what I think it was?"

I nod. There are tears in my eyes and I don't trust myself to say anything.

She sighs.

"But you got away."

"How long for?" I ask. Angrily I wipe a tear away that has leaked down my cheek. "You know, for a few days…out there…I forgot I was what I am. For years I was just rolling along in my rut, not thinking, just doing as I was told, getting by. Then for a few days, the world turned upside down."

The tears have gone now. I'm just angry.

"Now they're trying to put the world back the way it was. And I don't want that. I don't know how I'm going to live with it a day longer."

[24]

I DON'T KNOW HOW I get to sleep with all those thoughts whirling around my head, but I do eventually. I wake early and go out for a walk to try to get them into order.

Last night still haunts me, but Sherman was drunk. He has never been like that before. He will probably be as cocky as ever this morning. If he mentions it at all, he'll just laugh it off. And I'm not really surprised by Lee. He's just made it clear what he's always thought. There's just a part of me that's...disappointed.

I put that behind me though, because I've got a bigger problem to solve and that's how to get Julius out of prison. It needs to happen fast before they start to hurt him. It sounds like they're keeping Livia alive just to keep him going. I need to do this as soon as possible.

I'm not really thinking about the danger. I'm thinking about the problem. That's all it is. I can get in, because I've already set up a reason to go back in to collect the bowl. As trivial as that may be, it gets me in. Now I just need something to get rid of his lordship, as Tinker calls him, so I can get Julius out of the cell. I've reset locks before, but I assume this one will be a tougher nut to crack. I'll check what tools I've got, see if Tinker has any or knows where any are.

So I've reduced the prison problem to needing to distract Kitson. That just leaves me with the problem of getting Julius out of the base.

I stop and look around me. I become aware that there's a soldier watching me. I must be doing something mysterious. I make like I haven't seen him and carry on walking. I'm scanning the perimeter wall as I go. Out of the corner of my eye, I see the soldier moving too. He's following me. No, surely I'm just paranoid and he's walking in the same direction. I reach a junction and take a left. I walk down fifty meters, then take another left. As I turn, I glance behind me. He's still coming, but more quickly now.

I speed up too. My heart is beating faster. This is all I need. Or maybe I should just act innocent. I've done nothing. Yet. Surely no one can have a go at me for walking around the base. That's it. I should just stop acting like he's tailing me.

I stop where I am. Turn around and walk back the way I came, like I'd just forgotten something. He's coming towards me. His head is tilted down, so his face is covered by the green beret. As he reaches me, he looks up. My mouth drops.

It's Singer.

"I've been looking for you since yesterday," he says.

My mouth works, but my brain doesn't for a moment.

"Yesterday?" I say.

"Yeah, we got here yesterday. I snuck in and have been trying to find you."

"How did you get in?"

"I've got a token that'll get me past the guards. We've got some good techs in the Rads, you know. You'd fit in."

"But what are you doing here? We thought you'd be miles away by now."

"We couldn't leave J in here. They'll kill him. We gotta bust him and Livia out."

"It's too late for Livia. There's nothing they can do for her."

"Is she - ?"

"No. They've fixed up her wounds, but her blood is infected like you said. I think they're only keeping her alive to give Julius something to live for."

"Do you know how he is?"

"I know things are about to get a lot worse for him. He's resisted interrogation so far. Now I think the gloves are about to come off."

"We've got to get him out."

"My thoughts exactly. I had some ideas for the prison, but I didn't know what to do once I got him into the base."

"You can leave that to us. As you see, I can get inside and we can set up a diversion outside or inside too. We can make sure there's chaos in here. They'll be looking to stop people getting in then, not getting out."

"How can you do that with just three of you?"

He winks.

"We've got caches, remember? Little honeypots all over the woods. You just get him out here."

"Okay."

I'm thinking quickly now.

"Do something just after 6pm. Can you do that?"

"Sure. But make it count. We got just one shot at this."

I leave Singer. My mind is whirling again and my heart is beating twice as fast as normal. I can't believe I'm doing this, but things are just moving and I'm going with them.

I head straight for my room. I'm almost there when Sherman comes out of the shower. He's just wearing a towel and his toned chest is bare. He pauses when he sees me, scowls.

"Hi Sherman," I say, as neutrally as I can.

"I need some breakfast. I missed it in the mess."

"Okay. I'll get you something."

I go to keep on walking to my room.

"Kitchen's the other way," he says. He's not smiling.

"I was just getting something from my room."

"I'm hungry. My breakfast is first."

I see how this is. Master-servant. I'm getting punished because he didn't get what he wanted last night.

I turn on my heel and head for the kitchen. It's in the next block. I make him a bowl of oatmeal and make up some powdered egg to go with a couple of the hard tack biscuits that go with everything up here. Soon I'm coming back with the tray. I take it down to his room.

He's dressed now.

"Put it on the table."

I do so.

"Can I go now?" I ask.

"Take these with you," he says thrusting out his hand with his boots. "I want these cleaned by the time I've eaten."

I take them and leave before I say any of the things that are on the edge of my tongue and make everything a lot worse.

I've been polishing shoes for that family for years. I have them back to him before he's finished eating. I hope he's not intending to keep me busy all day, or I'll never get a chance to do anything. So I'll take the chance while I can.

I finally get to my locker to see what tools I've got. There are a few basic ones that I always carry and that are good for most ordinary jobs. And the splitter. The last splitter I had from the sawmill. I weigh it up in my hand, an idea forming for how I can use it. I might just have solved another problem.

[25]

SHERMAN THROWS JOBS AT ME all day. His uniform has developed a tear that needs to be mended, some clean clothes need to be washed, dried and pressed again. They don't keep me busy all day, but they break into it, stopping me from having long periods of time to myself.

To my surprise, this turns out to be helpful. The mindless jobs give me time to think in between moments of action. I mainly need time to think. This afternoon, I need to be back in the kitchen. During a couple of breaks, I go to the main canteen and manage to beg a few ingredients. While I'm there, I filch a couple more that I see lying around.

I start to cook at lunchtime. I want it to cook all afternoon so the flavors infuse. I'm good at disguising poor food with a great sauce.

At 5.30pm, I'm ready. I carry a tray over. It has a large pot and a small pot.

"I hope you enjoyed your dinner yesterday, lieutenant."

"As a matter of fact, I did," he says.

"Good. Because I brought you another one tonight. You should eat it while it's hot. I made something a lot simpler for him," I say, gesturing dismissively with my head towards the inside of the prison block.

I lay out cutlery and a glass the way I saw Tinker do it. I portion out the stew onto the buttery mashed potato. The steam rises and with it goes the smell. I can see I have Kitson's interest.

"That does smell good."

"Thank you. The secret is in the herbs. The army chefs don't know what to do with them. When I cook for my officer, he just bolts it down. It's a pleasure cooking for someone who knows their food."

"I'm sure it is," he says. He looks at his watch. "It's rather early."

"I'm sorry, is it?

"Ah well you've put it out now."

He pulls up the chair and sits down. He holds his nose over it and inhales. Then he picks up the fork and has a taste.

"Thyme...and mustard?" he says.

"Yes," I say.

"Does this have wine in?" he asks with surprise.

"In my dreams. I had to make do with a good stock."

He's enjoying it now. I start to go into the corridor to see Julius, then make as if I'd forgotten the doors were locked.

"Oh yeah," I say as if to myself.

For a moment, I don't think he's noticed.

"What are you doing?"

"I was going to go in while you were eating, then I forgot I can't."

He hasn't taken the bait. He's still eating. This was always the risk. I move around so I'm just in his line of sight. I want to irritate him while he's eating. It works, he sees me.

"It's okay. I can wait," I say.

He takes another mouthful, but I can see I'm taking the edge off his dinner. No one likes to be watched while they're eating. He stands suddenly.

"I'll let you through."

"Oh would you? Thanks. No need to rush. I'll just wait in there til you've digested."

He lets me through the three sets of doors. I watch his fingers again. The pass code hasn't changed and they still all have the same one. Then I'm through. I stay stood in the doorway where I'm out the way of the cameras. If I stay against the wall and under them, I won't appear in them. Julius looks at me, but I stay against the wall and point to the camera above my head. Now he knows I'm up to something.

The guy in cell 2 is still there. He's lying on his bunk. Perfect. I cast my eye over the camera again. The cabling is all visible and is typical of a jacked up installation. I need to work quickly. Keeping out of sight of the camera opposite Julius' cell, I pull out the cable from it, quickly swap in the splitter and make a circuit with the receiver from cell 2's camera. All done. As simple as that. Now if anyone looks at footage of Julius' cell, they'll just see footage of cell 2.

I step towards the cell and look back at the camera. The red light is still on! It should be off. Why isn't it working?

I duck back out of sight, but it's too late. My face is going to show up on the camera. I look at the cabling again. I don't know how I can have done it, but I must have unplugged the camera and plugged it straight in again. The splitter cable is still hanging there. I can't believe I did that. What do I do now? Is there any point in fixing it? Should I just get out now while I can, take the splitter with me and not even do this at all?

Then I think of what they're going to do with Julius. I look at his face. They've already started doing something to him. There are cuts and bruises on it. It's not bad, but they've started to soften him up. And then there's Singer and the others about to let off something outside. There are four other lives on the line, not just mine.

But if they know I was involved in this, my life's on the line too. I make a snap decision. I keep going. Everything has been pointing to this: the way they're treating Julius and Livia, Sherman's and Lee's attitude towards me, the way I felt when we were in the forest.

I fix the splitter properly this time. It probably doesn't matter anymore, but at least I don't feel like I'm being watched. Then I start on the lock on the cell. First I try Kitson's standard four digit code.

It doesn't work.

I'm disappointed, but it seems he has some sense after all. So now the only way around will be with tools.

I don't have long; the lieutenant will be along any minute. This has been such a gamble, because I don't know what kind of lock they have and whether it is one I can override. I pop the panel off the lock mechanism.

It's great news. Seems like I was right to rely on this being a temporary base set up in the wilds. They've been working on 'good enough' and that's good enough to keep the doors closed with prisoners inside, but not good enough to stop tampering.

So I start to tamper. I have to fool the system into thinking I've got the master key by by-passing the key. I'm sweating and I can feel my heart beating. At the same time, I'm listening out for the door opening behind me. This is very fiddly work. I have to get two tools inside a small cavity and I'm pressing my head against the wall to try to see what I'm doing because there's only a certain amount you can do by feel.

"Come on," I say to myself. I can feel my tongue is poking out with concentration. I don't know what Julius is doing. My hand slips and I curse. I need to try again. I'm having to get in behind the code core and make a connection on the rear so that I can trip that as if the code had been entered.

"Mouse!" Julius hisses in warning.

At the same moment, I hear the door open behind me. I turn and see Kitson's shocked face as he sees me, then a metal pan lid comes spinning out of the cell, thrown by Julius. It hits the lieutenant square on the nose. At the same time, I barrel into him. I'm not big, but I hit him with the full weight of my body. He's already off balance from the lid and this pushes him back against the bars. Julius doesn't waste any time. He has his fingers around the man's neck and is pressing into it. Kitson's eyes are bulging. He's grabbing at Julius' fingers.

"Don't kill him!" I say.

Julius doesn't reply. He's putting all his effort into strangling Kitson. Suddenly he goes limp. Julius holds onto the lieutenant a moment longer, then lets go. Kitson slumps to the ground.

"Is he dead?" I ask. I'm shocked at what I've just seen.

"I don't know. Get on with the lock or we both will be though."

I don't need to be told twice. I go back to the panel. It only takes me a couple of seconds and the door of the cell slides open. Julius drops to his knees and feels for a pulse.

"He's in luck. He's just unconscious. Now then, I hope you can get us through those other doors."

"That's easy," I say.

He pulls the sidearm out of the lieutenant's holster. I tap in the code on the first door and we're through. I do the same thing on the next two and we're out in the front office, the lieutenant's bowl is on his desk, practically licked clean.

"Now we just need to wait for Singer," I say. "He's creating a diversion."

Julius looks at me, his eyes wide.

"How did you - ?"

"Not me. They followed you here."

"Where's Livia?"

"In the hospital."

"We need to get her out."

"Julius, we can't. I couldn't tell you properly before. The toxins are all through her. Her blood is completely contaminated. They were just keeping her alive to keep you going while they interrogated you. I'm so sorry."

He narrows his eyes, trying to get his mind around this.

"You said that to me before, but there's a way. They can save her."

"Julius, face it, they can't. We've got to get out of here."

"I'm not going without her. You don't have to come, just tell me where the hospital is."

I look at my watch. We still have nearly twenty minutes before it's six o'clock. Maybe if he sees her, he'll understand the state she's in because I can't seem to get it across in words.

The lieutenant's beret is on his desk. I hand it to Julius.

"Put this on. No one goes round bare headed out there. And put his coat on."

We walk outside. I feel a crazy urge to run, but I know we need to walk. Running will just draw attention to us. I must be insane. This is so slow. Surely we can walk a bit faster, but no, I manage to walk casually although every part of me is screaming to look behind me, to run, to hide, to do anything but walk calmly with an escaped prisoner down the road in an army base.

Yet it is working. Uniformed soldiers and the odd base worker walk past us as if we belong there. Neither of us speaks.

I can see the hospital in front of us. I walk in. I recognize the clerk on duty at the front from before. I wave as casually as I can.

"I know my way thanks," I say.

We walk on through.

Livia is in the room behind the glass. She is slowly pacing up and down, stretching her arms out behind her. There's another bored guard sitting next to the glass. He looks at Julius with mild interest.

"Livia," says Julius.

She had her back to the glass and she turns her pallid face towards us when she hears his voice.

"J!" she croaks. "You're here?"

I look at the guard. He's beginning to look puzzled. This is going to get ugly at any moment.

"Hey, you dropped something," says Julius.

The guard looks down instinctively and at the same moment, Julius whips the butt end of his pistol around, catching the guard on the side of the head. He tumbles off the chair onto the floor.

Julius turns his attention back to Livia.

"We're getting you out of here," he says.

"J, no. I'm dying. I'm already sick. Leave me and get out."

"I'm not leaving you. We can fix you. The nanomeds can fix you."

"They won't give them to me."

"I will. Come on."

He goes through the guard's pockets and quickly finds the token that opens the door.

In a few moments, he's changed into the guard's uniform. It's too short for him, but his boots disguise that enough for a casual observer. He puts the rifle over his shoulder and drags the unconscious guard into the room, out of sight below the glass.

"Get onto the bed," Julius says to Livia.

"But I can walk."

"Get on."

The bed is on wheels and he stands behind it ready to push.

"Right. Let's find the blood bank," he says.

We wheel her out into the corridor. Almost immediately we come across a nurse.

She looks surprised.

"We need to find the blood bank," I say.

"Oh. Down the back. Follow me."

Julius is looking down so his damaged face is not visible. We follow her down corridors. Sometimes a doctor, nurse or orderly passes us, but people barely look twice except to greet the nurse.

She pushes open the doors ahead of us and we're in a room with doors on either side. The door on the left is big and sealed. Through the window I can see blood bags, so we're in the right place. To the right are swing doors and a brightly lit room is visible through the round windows.

A man is sitting at a desk across the room. He turns around when he hears us enter.

"I wasn't expecting anyone," he said. "Who's this?"

The nurse turns to me for explanation. I turn to Julius. This is his show. I don't even know why I'm here.

"She needs a full transfusion," says Julius.

"Where's the authorization?" asks the doctor.

"Authorization?" says Julius.

"Well I can't do anything without an authorization. I don't even know who she is, what kind of blood."

"Nanomed blood," says Julius.

"Which type? What mixture? This is most unusual. Who sent you?"

He reaches for a perco unit on his desk.

"Don't do that," says Julius. He's pulled out the pistol he took from Kitson. He waves it at the nurse, gesturing for her to move around so that she is next to the doctor.

"There is no authorization, but you will do the transfusion. She has toxin-contaminated blood and you will replace it all with nanomeds."

"Do you know how dangerous that is?"

"Not as dangerous as not having it. She'll die."

"But you can't just give her nanomeds. It's not as simple as that. You need to determine the balance for her metabolism, you need to program them with her DNA."

"We don't have time for that."

"There are different types: builders, cleaners, killers, markers. They replicate the body's natural defenses. Get that balance wrong and you're putting her life at risk."

"Just give her a standard mixture. Her life is already at risk."

"It's my job to preserve life."

"So preserve it," Julius says. He raises the gun.

"Kill me and you won't get the transfusion," says the doctor.

He's brave, I'll say that for him.

"If I kill you, you won't be alive any more. She's already dying. Do it," says Julius.

He stares grimly at the doctor. "I'll count to five," he says. "One. Two. Three."

"All right. I'll do it. Do you know her blood type? We can at least get that right."

"O."

"That's a good start then. Nurse, please can you prep her with a saline."

He turns to Julius.

"I will need to go into the blood room."

It is as much a question as a statement. Julius nods and waves him in. He follows him into the blood room. I wheel Livia into the operating theatre.

"Just put her here," says the nurse. She is very flustered. "Are you okay?"

For a moment, I think she's talking to Livia, then I realize she's talking to me. She assumes I've been taken hostage by Julius as well. I nod.

"Who is he?" she asks. I shrug and shake my head.

"You know this could take a couple of hours," she says.

A couple of hours? I don't have that time!

"The doctor could speed it up if he uses the ICP," she adds.

"What's that?"

"It's an intravenous pump."

"How long would that take?"

"It could still take an hour."

"I think we just need to do what he says," I suggest.

She pulls on some medical gloves from a box on the side, swabs Julia's arm and inserts a needle.

At that moment, Julius and the doctor return. The doctor is carrying an armful of blood bags. He lays these out, then turns to Julius, his hands out, imploring.

"Look, I know who you are and I'm asking you again not to do this."

Julius walks right up to him and looks down at him.

"I heard you the first time. If you can have that tech, she can have that tech. She gets the tech. Just. Do it."

"Okay. On your head be it."

"Fine. Do it."

The nurse prepares the bag of saline solution and fixes the tube to the needle in Livia's skin.

"This bag first," says the doctor. He picks up one of the blood bags, opens it and hands it to the nurse who hangs it next to the saline.

"Last chance," says the doctor.

"Yours too," says Julius without looking at him.

The doctor nods at the nurse who switches tubes on the bags so that now the new blood is going into Livia.

"Now we wait," says the doctor.

"I know this is going to take a very long time," I say pointedly. "Even with an ICP it could take an hour, couldn't it?"

The doctor looks at me. The nurse frowns, presumably because I just gave useful information to "the enemy".

"Well if it can get us all out of here faster..." I say.

"What's an ICP?" asks Julius.

"It's sometimes used under battlefield conditions when we need to move people quickly. It's a pump that allows the body to accept the new blood at a faster rate."

"Perfect," says Julius. "Use it. Why didn't you think of it before?"

"It's less comfortable for the patient because it's quite invasive."

"Livia?" asks Julius.

"Anything to get us out of here faster," she says.

The doctor points at the cupboard.

"May I?"

"I'm watching," says Julius.

The doctor opens the cupboard and pulls out a metal box about the size of a toaster. He sets it on a small wheeled table next to the bed. He prepares Livia's other arm and fixes a metal tube about the length of my little finger into it.

"This will hurt," he says.

He inserts the tube into a vein. I see her wince as it goes in.

"Okay?" he says to her.

She nods.

He fixes two plates to her chest over her heart.

"What is that doing?" Livia asks.

"It speeds up your heart to increase blood flow," he says. "The nanomeds themselves will also facilitate the process."

Then we hear an explosion.

It must be Singer and the others. They've started their attack and we're in here in the middle of a long medical procedure.

"What's that?" says the nurse.

A siren sounds.

"Should we get under cover?" she asks.

"No. Keep going," says Julius.

"There's nothing more we need to do apart from swap the bags over when they're empty," says the doctor.

The noise outside is louder than I would have expected, but these are not proper buildings and I guess the prefab walls are thinner than more permanent ones would be.

We hear a copter taking off. There's shouting.

With that, we all lapse into silence. The only sound from in here is the humming of the ICP. The doctor monitors a display. Outside there is still a siren, occasionally some gunfire.

I am beside myself. Singer's diversion is in full swing and we're in here all standing still.

I watch the blood going in. It looks like normal blood to me, just as red as anyone else's, but I know that inside it there are little machines. I have no idea what nanomeds even look like. I always imagine them like small insects, swimming through the veins and arteries on little metal legs.

"How do you feel?" I ask Livia.

"A bit weird."

"Bad weird?"

"Good weird. I think."

"I would feel weird with tiny metal robots filling my body," I say.

"They're not metal," says the doctor as if I'm an idiot. "They're organic compounds, adapted human cells."

The nurse replaces one of the bags. We wait some more.

There's another explosion and we hear machine gun fire.

"It sounds serious," says the nurse looking startled.

"They wouldn't attack a hospital," says Julius. "They leave that to government troopers."

"Your story," says the doctor.

"Whatever you say," says Julius.

The nurse changes another bag.

It's strange being in here listening to what's going on outside, wondering what could be happening. Singer, Rash and Double could all be dead now. They were our chance to get out in the confusion. I stare hard at Julius, willing him to look at me. For a moment, he does. Then he looks away and stares fixedly at Livia. Does he have another plan? Singer was all I had and that was going to be about finding some sort of opportunity. It wasn't even a good plan.

Then all of a sudden it's over. There's no more firing. The explosions have stopped. We can still hear the copter passing overhead now and then, presumably circling the base and the surroundings.

Another bag.

"How are you feeling?" Julius asks his sister. She just looks at him and nods, then she turns back to the bag of nanomed blood. She watches it seeping into her arm.

I half expect her to change, be different somehow. Maybe I think she's going to leap off the bed and be, well, superhuman. Instead she just lies there watching the new blood go into her.

Then there's a sound. Voices. Footsteps. Someone is coming.

Two soldiers burst in carrying a wounded comrade between them. The front of his jacket is a bloody mess, his head lolls around. There's an orderly behind. They stop, take in the scene very quickly. Julius has instinctively raised his pistol. Perhaps if he had not done that, we would have got away with it. At least for a few more minutes.

He waves the four of them in.

"What's going on here?" demands one of the troopers.

"Never mind," says Julius.

"He needs blood," the trooper says.

Julius looks at the nurse and nods.

"Put him on that gurney," she says, indicating a low, folded down stretcher on wheels.

"You should give yourself up," says the doctor. "This can't last."

This time Julius does not respond to him.

I am frozen with fear and disappointment. I'm so stupid. I didn't think this through at all.

"Can I see his tag?" the nurse asks. One of the troopers slips the dog tag from around the injured man's neck. She scans it and hands it back.

"I need to get some blood," she says to Julius.

He nods. It's the nod of a man resigned to his fate. It's the nod of a man who has gambled and lost.

When troopers burst into the room a few minutes later with their weapons raised, he does not respond. He simply carefully places the pistol on the bed and unshoulders the rifle. When he is taken away, I am taken with him. They must have found the video footage or Kitson has come around.

However they found out, it is all over for me too.

[26]

WE ARE MARCHED ACROSS THE base. I look to see if I can work out what happened during the attack. The most obvious sign is one of the watch towers has had much of its top blown off. There are a few bullet holes in some of the buildings on the sides that face the outside. Beyond that, I can see little damage. I half expected there to be bodies, but the wounded trooper who was brought into the hospital is the only injury I have seen so far. I wonder what happened to Singer, Double and Rash.

I can't believe this is happening. Everything had been going smoothly, incredibly smoothly, until Julius decided to rescue Livia. How could he have risked everything? How could he decide to start a lengthy medical procedure when time was of the essence? My world has come crumbling down. I am numb. I am bitter. Yet at the same time, I can't really blame Julius. I walked into this with eyes wide open. How could I even think there was a chance it would work?

Now I don't want to think about what could be waiting for me: execution, imprisonment or at best, the rest of my life in a work camp. Either way, it won't be a long life. I won't need to worry about a home any more. I've blown all that.

I didn't really consider the risks of what I was doing. I was carried along by the moment. It is hard to think about what I might have done if I had thought about it more. If I had known it would have ended like this, then of course I would have done nothing. It had seemed like the right thing to do. Circumstances directed me to do it. I felt like I had no other choice.

So maybe I was right. Maybe this is just the way out for me.

We enter a building. I have not been able to look at Julius. Livia is still in the hospital. I don't know what they are doing to her. Perhaps they are draining the blood out of her, taking their nanomeds back.

We are marched along a corridor, around a corner, down another corridor. I am directed into a room, Julius into another. In the room is a table with a chair on either side. I am told to sit in one of the chairs. A trooper comes into the room with me and stands by the door. He has a pistol and a truncheon. The door is shut. I don't know where they are taking Julius, but I assume it is to another room like this one. They are going to interrogate us.

I have been sat in here for about half an hour when the door opens. The Colonel comes in. I have not seen him since we first arrived at the base. I had almost forgotten he was up here at all. The guard salutes. Colonel Hammond closes the door behind him, then stands looking down at me for a few moments. I don't know what to do with myself. Should I look defiant or remorseful? Should I smile and say hello.

When he does sit down, he still says nothing, but looks across the table at me. I wish he would say something, then I would have something to respond to.

Finally, he speaks.

"So what do you have to say for yourself?"

I was not expecting that question. In my confusion about what to say, I still know I need to be careful about what I do say. I don't know what they know and I could easily incriminate myself. It feels like the kind of question they would have asked me at school – did ask me at school – when I had misbehaved.

"I didn't mean it to happen," I say.

"And what were you doing?"

"I heard that Livia was dying, sir. I wanted Julius to be able to see her before she died. Before he died."

"And what business was that of yours?"

"I have no family, sir. So I see family as important. They are brother and sister, sir."

"And this sympathy was enough to lead you to commit treason? You do realize what you did was treasonous, don't you?"

"No sir. I didn't think about it like that."

I'm wrong-footed by his approach. I expected something harsher.

"What did he offer you?" he asks.

"Offer me, sir? Nothing."

He looks like he doesn't believe me. That's not surprising. What fool would do something like that for nothing? I wonder if I should try to explain my motives. Would he care? Would he even understand? But then some of those motives are treasonous because they're about the place of redbloods in society. Some of my reasons were political. How can I help that, I am a redblood. I have no rights except the ones the bluebloods deign to let me have until they take them away from me again.

"What were you going to do after he had spoken to his sister?"

Until he asks this question, it hasn't occurred to me that I could pretend that escape wasn't part of my plan.

"I just assumed he would be caught," I say. My voice is quiet.

"Both of you?"

"No. I was hoping no one would know I was involved. That I could just melt away after he had seen his sister. They were both going to die anyway."

He contemplates me. He is trying to see if I am telling the truth. Surely it's obvious I'm lying.

"How did Dexter communicate with the Rads outside?"

"Dexter?" I ask.

"Julius," he says. "Julius Dexter."

"When do you mean?" I ask. He must be talking about Singer's raid.

"How did he coordinate the raid?"

I make my eyes go wide.

"Was that what I heard when we were inside the hospital? And then I saw the tower. The Rads. I would never have thought..." I trail off, not wanting to talk too much.

"It looks very suspicious that the Rads attack us at the same time that you have broken Dexter out of his cell."

"I suppose it does," I say, trying to look as though I'm just seeing this. "I don't know." I'm trying to sound innocent, but I don't think I sound very convincing.

"But you're a comms specialist. What did you give him to communicate with the Rads?"

"Nothing!" I say immediately, my acting helped enormously because here I am telling the truth. Would he believe a Rad had been moving freely about his base anyway?

"And I'm not a comms specialist. I hardly know anything really."

He raises an eyebrow.

"You know enough to be dangerous," he says. "How did you get into the prison cells? There are three coded doors."

"It wasn't the lieutenant's fault," I say. "I just watched his hand on the keys."

That raised eyebrow again.

"You watched his hand?"

"Yes," I say simply.

"On three doors? And remembered three codes?"

I could get Kitson into trouble for his poor security protocols. I suspect he's in enough trouble as it is. I just nod.

The Colonel is giving me no indication whether he has believed any of my story. I haven't had time to think about whether it fits together anyway. And then there's Julius. Will his story match mine? Will he even give a story? Was there anything in what I said that could endanger Julius? But no, that doesn't matter. Surely I can't make it any worse for him than it already is.

"Second lieutenant Hammond and Cadet Hammond told me that you spent a good deal of time talking to Dexter while you were held captive."

"I spent some time talking to him, sir. I don't know if it was all that much. Most of the time we were just walking."

That's the truth too.

"What did you talk about?" he asks.

"He told me what they were fighting for. He said they wanted the nanomeds too. They want to be bluebloods."

"And what do you think about that?"

Careful now.

"It surprised me. I always thought they just wanted to destroy us. Create anarchy."

"And them having nanomeds would be anarchy, wouldn't it?" says the Colonel. "Everyone can't be the same. The different bloods perform different functions in our society. Redbloods wouldn't do the valuable work they do because they would want to be bluebloods. But you need to earn that status. Frankly, you need to pay for that status. Nanomeds aren't cheap. Where would we be if everyone had them?"

"And who would look after *them*?" I say. I think it can't hurt to support the Colonel in his self-justification.

"Who?"

"The redbloods. Well, at the moment, the bluebloods look after us. I don't think you'd do that if we had blue blood too. You'd expect us to fend for ourselves."

"That's true."

For a moment, he almost looks benevolent. And in a way, it is true for me. I really don't know where I would be if I hadn't been taken in by the Hammonds. As a vagrant, it is hard to find a job and even harder to survive as a child. So I am grateful to the Hammonds, but suddenly I feel angry that I need to be grateful.

"So did Dexter influence you? Corrupt your thinking?"

I don't like to think of it like that. No matter how doomed Julius already is, I struggle to load more crimes onto him. I can't say that he corrupted my thinking.

"He told me things that made me think differently, sir. I guess I was confused."

"So confused that you decided you would break him out of prison."

I decide not to respond to that one. He takes my silence as assent anyway.

"It is collaboration with the enemy and a treasonable offence, potentially punishable by death."

Even if I wanted to respond to that, I can't bring my mouth to say anything. I could say that I'm sorry, but I'm not sorry. At least, I'm not remorseful about what I did, I'm just sorry that I'm in this mess, sorry that I failed to plan.

"You do realize how serious this is don't you?"

I look down.

He nods brusquely and gets up to leave. I watch him go and sit looking at the closed door for several minutes before another guard comes to take me to a cell.

[27]

I HAVE BEEN PUT IN a cell. It is ironic to be back in the prison block. There is no sign of the lieutenant. Perhaps he is in hospital or perhaps he has been disciplined. I'm relieved he is not there. I tricked him and no one likes to be tricked. I would not want him as my jailor.

I have nothing to do. No one tries to give me anything to do. So for three days, I'm sitting in here or pacing up and down. I think of just about every possible scenario for what could happen to me. I think of numerous ways they could execute me: hanging, firing squad. I don't think they would torture me. There's no information I could give them apart from a true version of what really happened and that's not worth anything to them. It could be prison, but why waste prison on me when they could put me to work doing something useful to the state?

I exercise for something to do. I do press ups, squats, running on the spot. When I'm not doing that, I can't stop thinking, so I do as much sleeping as I can.

It's early morning when they come for me. I'm convinced it's my execution. Those always happen first thing in the morning.

They cuff me and take me outside, marching me between the buildings. The sky is clear and the morning air is fresh. I suck it in. This last air I will ever breathe tastes beautiful. It tastes of trees and the damp earth. It tastes of the mountains. I look towards them, but they are hidden by the trees.

I notice everything: the vehicle tracks on the ground, the texture of the prefabricated buildings, the bent blade of grass in a bare patch of soil that I walk past. I see the creases on the jacket of the guard in front of me. I study the way it bunches and the light and dark of the cloth merely caused by the light and wonder whether I could draw such a thing.

We round a corner. I expect to see a gallows or a firing squad lined up waiting.

Instead, there's a copter.

It's like the one I came north on. So it's not a death sentence yet. They're taking me somewhere.

Standing at the corner of the building is another surprise: Lee. He is looking very stern, but he puts his hand out to the guard for us to stop. He walks over to us.

I look at him quizzically. He looks very uncomfortable. He is looking away, but then he drags his eyes onto me.

"I don't know what's going to happen to you," he says. "I tried to find out."

Then he hesitates. He seems confused. It's very odd. I just want him to let me go on to wherever it is I'm going. Then he speaks again.

"I hope I see you again."

He looks at me then. He looks me right in the eyes. I know I'm frowning at him. There seems to be more that he wants to say. He holds my eyes for another beat, then looks away.

The guard gives me a prod and I set off again, but I look over my shoulder at Lee. He is still watching me. The guard prods me again and guides me inside the copter and indicates a seat. I take it and the guard takes the one next to me.

Before I can think any more about that exchange with Lee, another figure darkens the doorway. It's Sherman. He's carrying his pack. He hesitates as he boards and looks at me with a strange expression. He at least has the decency to look awkward. I am surprised when he comes and sits on the other side of me. I feel uncomfortable.

The copter's engines start up and the vibration runs down the body of the aircraft. There is another soldier in the doorway. He turns to talk to someone I can't see, beckons.

Livia climbs in through the doorway. She looks much better than she did in hospital. Her cheeks have color and she's walking well. Her eyes light up for a moment, but then she just nods at me and I nod back.

Another man climbs aboard. It is Julius. Unbelievably, his swagger has returned. He turns and smiles at the guards behind him, then saunters over to a seat. He did not wait to be told where to go, but he has chosen one diagonally opposite to Livia and the guards seem comfortable with that.

"It's a reunion," says Sherman under his breath.

Julius surveys everyone in the copter, taking us all in. His eyes pause for a moment on me and I think I detect a greeting in them, but he is being careful about showing any familiarity. I still don't know what he said under interrogation, assuming he said anything at all. I look at him out of the corner of my eye. There are no fresh bruises on his face, but he looks drawn and pale. It's hardly surprising. His future can't be anything but much more unpleasant than mine and probably shorter.

This copter is busier than the one on which I flew north. There are five guards. Livia and Julius have two each to my one. I almost feel offended. I think we are about to leave, but one more person climbs in through the hatch. It is the Colonel. All the guards and Sherman stand up and salute. He returns the salute and drops into a seat.

A soldier pokes his head into the doorway, takes a quick look around the cabin, then closes the hatch. The engine noise picks up again and I feel us lift off. I twist to look out of the window as the base drops away. Lee is still there watching us leave, but soon he and the base have gone and we're rapidly gaining height. I feel heavy in my seat.

We are over the trees now and I have a brief glimpse of the mountains before the copter turns and all I can see are trees.

I turn back and glance up and down the cabin. Colonel Hammond is paging through a tab, catching up on paperwork. Julius and Livia seem lost in their own thoughts and the guards look like they are in neutral, yet ready to pounce. One sits opposite each of their charges, while the other sits a seat away, quarter turned towards them.

I become lost in my thoughts too about how different this is to my previous flight. Then, everything was before me. Now it is all behind me, done and dusted. I did not know what to expect from my time at Borealis Base, but it certainly was not anything like this.

Once more, my mind whirls around what will become of me. My destiny was never my own, but there have been times, like when I was a vagrant, when it was more mine than others'. But now, I have no control at all and that is frightening. Anything could happen to me and there's nothing I can do about it. I feel as though I have stopped being a person.

From time to time, Sherman shifts in his seat beside me. It is at least an hour since he made his comment about it being a reunion when he speaks again. He speaks quietly so that no one else can hear us above the sound of the engine. The military seem to put minimal sound-proofing in their copters.

"I'm not a total ass," he says.

There would seem to be more, so I wait. Is this supposed to be an apology for how he has behaved towards me?

"We didn't talk about everything you did while we were out there. They talked to us separately and both of us just told them about the good things."

"Thank you," I say, because that seems to be right thing to say. I assume he is talking about their debriefing. This would suggest they did not mention what I did to help the Rads at the sawmill, although admittedly they don't know the half of what I did or what I enabled the Rads to do.

"We did tell them you tried to help us escape."

I nod. It isn't much, but it is something. Both of them, Lee and Sherman, seem to have tried to paint me in a positive light, or at least, a less negative light. I am grateful for that. This means that the only thing they have over me is busting Julius out of prison. Not that this is small, but it is better.

What worries me is that Sherman and Lee may think they have something over me. They could blackmail me. Actually, that doesn't worry me about Lee. I don't think he would do anything like that. I don't know why, it's just a gut feeling and I've always trusted those, ever since I was on the street.

But Sherman? I don't trust Sherman and I especially don't trust him after what happened in his room.

"Was it because of me that you did it?" he asks.

It's as if he's reading my thoughts.

"Yeah, partly," I say.

He grunts. "Thought so," he said.

It does have to be about him, doesn't it? Well, I can pander to that if it helps paint my actions in a more excusable light.

"They sending you back early?" I ask.

He grunts again.

"This flight was going and the Colonel reckoned I'd learned more than enough for one assignment."

He laughs and pulls out a tab and starts to play a game.

"Do you know - " I start, then I look at the Colonel, but he is engrossed in his work. Sherman stops playing and looks at me. "Do you know what's going to happen to me?"

"I said we put in a good word for you," he says. "I don't know. Maybe a work camp. I don't know."

At least he has the decency to find it an awkward subject to talk about. He returns to his game and I return to staring into space and trying to stop thinking.

I'm still like that as we fly in over the city. I feel like I've been away a long time. It is odd to see nothing but buildings and roads. I had become used to the wilderness.

The military base comes closer and we drop towards it, losing height. Then we are touching down and the hatch opens.

My brief period in limbo has ended. Now comes what comes.

[28]

ONE BY ONE WE LEAVE the copter. We stand beside the aircraft, waiting. Livia is looking nervous, Julius less so, but I think I see it in the way his eyes dart about briefly as he checks out the new environment.

Three vehicles draw up. There is a white truck which has armored sides and two smaller more lightly armored trucks. A soldier from the larger truck climbs out of the cab and opens up the door at the back. Our guards lead us over.

So I'm going into a prison van. Livia climbs up first, then Julius. I am about to follow, but the lead guard shakes his head and points to one of the smaller vehicles.

"No room for you. Get in the soft-top."

Again, I'm forced to find solace in not being treated as a high risk criminal. Two soldiers follow Livia and Julius in. I just see them being secured before I am moved on.

Two guards and Sherman climb in with me, the Colonel and the last guard climb in the other soft-top, as the guard called it. Then we pull off.

"Where are we going?" I ask.

"Rockfield," says the guard.

I should have guessed. It's the high security prison. We set off, driving through the base. Barriers open for us as we go and soon we are out on the highway. We are in front, the armored truck behind us with the Colonel's soft-top taking up the rear.

We are making good speed, but traffic becomes heavier as we go closer to the central city. I know we'll need to pass the western edge of it.

"Accident ahead," says the driver, relaying something he's hearing through his headset. We can see the traffic is thickening in front of us and moving more slowly.

"Roger that," says the driver into his perco. He takes an exit and all three vehicles drive off the main highway and into urban streets. Traffic is lighter and I look out of the window at a normality that now looks alien to me. This is a redblood neighborhood. The buildings look tired and in need of some attention, but the streets are full of people going about their business.

We stop at an intersection. There is a shop, the kind of shop I used to go into as a kid to sell unusual but useful things that I had come across. A woman watches us go by, her face blank. I wonder what she is thinking.

We drive on. We are among blocky buildings housing light industry now and there is no one about, just a few trucks. A large one is backing out of the building in front of us. The driver does not appear to have seen us. Our driver sounds his siren, but the truck keeps coming and we are forced to stop.

Suddenly there is a thunderous crash from behind us and our truck bucks forward. I feel like my entire body has been hit by a huge sledgehammer. My head pounds and my ears are ringing, my leg is wet. Dazed, I turn to look at my guard who is leaning forward strangely. There is something sticking out of the back of his head. He is not moving.

There is another noise. I'm still struggling to take in what is going on. I can't think properly. It's a rapid noise.

I work out what is going on. A machine gun is firing. We are under attack. My brain feels like it is working very slowly, yet very little time has passed since this experience started. I don't understand why we are under attack. We are in the city.

In the front seat, the driver and Sherman are tipping off their seats and out of their doors. The guard next to me grabs my arm and pulls me. As I reach the doorway, he spins around, letting go of me and falls to the ground. Unbalanced, I fall out of the vehicle and land beside him. There is a spreading red patch below his right shoulder and he is mouthing things at me that I cannot hear.

"Keep down!" shouts a voice. It might be Sherman. It could be anyone. Looking around to trace it, I see the armored truck. The front of it has been ripped apart. There is something that could be the driver in the remains of the cab.

There is more gunfire. I can't see where it is coming from. There seems to be more than one source.

A flash of white light and afterwards another roar. I feel pummeled again. The explosion was behind the armored truck.

"They got Dad's truck!"

It's the voice again. It is coming from right beside me. Sherman is there. He has blood on his face and dust in his hair. I'm trying to understand why he looks different to a few moments ago.

All of a sudden, there are people in the street, people with guns and balaclavas which mask their faces. A spray of bullets riddles the truck above me. Had I not been lying on the ground, I think I would be dead.

I can see the man who fired. He looked in our direction when he pointed his gun at us. There is something familiar about the masked man next to him. He is very tall and broad, but I can't think who he is.

More firing.

Flames are coming from behind the truck. It must be the other soft-top. The people in balaclavas are retreating across the road. Our driver is returning fire with his pistol now. He is kneeling beside our soft-top. Sherman has picked up a rifle from the guard on the ground and is also firing. Suddenly, our vehicle becomes a target for those attacking us. Somehow the Rads have mounted a rescue. I wonder if they know I'm here. I wonder if they care.

Bullets thud into the soft-top. I look at the prison truck. It's much more solid and will provide more cover. I just want to get away from where I am. They're focusing on the front of our vehicle where the driver is. He ducks down to reload.

I look at the distance between the soft-top and the truck. Could I make it? The driver is ramming a new magazine into his pistol and is firing again. Maybe that will be enough distraction.

Almost before I realize it myself, I'm up and running across the gap. As I reach the truck it feels like someone has just pushed me over and I fall sprawling, but I am behind the truck. I look back expecting to see someone there to have pushed me, but there is no one. I put my hand up to rub the bruise and I feel my shoulder is wet. I look at my hand and there is blood on it. It takes a moment to register that I have been shot. I don't want to look at it. It doesn't hurt. I think looking at it might change that.

I hunker down behind the wheel. Sherman is too intent on firing and keeping out of sight to notice I've gone. I glance at the other soft-top. It's the first time I have looked at it since the attack started. It was probably less than a minute ago, but it feels like an age. Both front wheels have blown off. There are flames around the front. My eye is caught by a little movement. Someone is half out of the side door; I can see a head and shoulders. It looks like the Colonel. He is not wearing his beret and his head is bleeding. Why is he still in there? He must be injured.

I need to help him. I don't really think about it. This is a man I have known for years. We are both under fire and we have both been shot by the same people. There is another gap between the front soft-top and the big truck which is currently shielding me. It is wider than the one I already ran across. I look back at Sherman and the driver. Both are leaning against the back of their vehicle. Neither is firing. I wonder if they are out of ammunition.

Then I hear noises coming from the rear of the truck. There are voices and bangs of something hard on metal which reverberates around to me. Someone is hitting the back doors of the truck.

I freeze. Running to what I thought was a safer place has just put me closer to the Rads. I press myself up against the wheel, praying no one looks around the side of the truck.

Someone shouts: "Clear!"

Seconds later there is a small explosion. One of the doors swings open and clangs against the back of the truck. Immediately, there are gunshots.

There is movement: shouting and scuffling from the rear of the truck.

I can use this moment of confusion to my advantage. I crawl along the side of the truck. When I reach the other wheel, I just run. Everything slows down.

I can't help but turn to look as I run, wanting to face my death, if it is coming. I take in everything in amazing detail. There is a group moving away from the rear of the truck and its open doors. Most of them have their backs to us and are wearing balaclavas. Two aren't. It is Julius and Livia and they are being led from the back of the big truck. They have their heads down and are running now.

One of the men with balaclavas turns as I run across the gap. He raises his gun with one hand and looses off a shot. I am looking him in the eye as he does it. I know those eyes even though I cannot see the rest of his face, but in that moment, I can't remember why.

Then I feel like both of my legs have been whacked out from under me with a bat. Once more I'm down on the ground. Once more I look back, expecting the masked gunman to be there to finish me, but he is not.

I am lying on my back and looking up. The Colonel is above me. His face is in profile and I can see he is still conscious, but only just. I try to stand, but my right leg won't seem to cooperate, so I pull myself up the side of the vehicle and peer inside.

I can see why the Colonel cannot get out. The soldier sat next to him was a big man. He has fallen across the Colonel and is either unconscious or dead. The Colonel has also fallen and cannot get out. I think he's been hit too.

Bullets are still pinging around us from where other Rads have vantage points. I grab the Colonel by the shoulders and pull, but nothing happens. He is wedged under the soldier.

I pull myself further up and haul myself half inside the truck. I am lying next to the Colonel and trying to push the soldier off him. He moves and I push his deadweight upright. As I do so, his whole body judders and a bullet explodes out of his back and into the seat. I wedge him upright, then slip back out and try again on the Colonel.

This time, he comes, slowly, but slides out, his passage lubricated by the blood coming out of his legs. I am standing now, but bent over, trying to stay low and out of sight. More bullets rake the car. I am knocked backwards with the Colonel on top of me.

I lie there dazed. There is a burning sensation in my chest. Several more explosions rock the vehicles. I feel the shock wave go over the top of me. Sound is cut off suddenly like it is coming from underground. We are showered by bits of grit and metal and other things I don't want to think about. My forehead is wet and I'm feeling faint. I try to move the Colonel off me, but the effort is too much.

[29]

I WAKE UP IN A lit room. The ceiling is white, the sheets are crisp. It is a few moments before it occurs to me that I do not know where I am. It is another few moments before I remember that there was an attack on the convoy and that I am a criminal with an uncertain future.

I remember being shot. I remember explosions. I was injured. I move my hand up to my shoulder. There is a slight bump of a healing wound, but no scab. How long have I been unconscious?

There were other injuries too. My leg. I struggle to remember what happened. I tried to pull the Colonel from the soft-top. I cannot remember what happened after that.

I push myself up in the bed and sit back. I look around. I am in a room on my own. There are two chairs on the other side of the room and a small table. There is also a narrow cupboard.

I consider getting up. I feel a little stiff, my leg has a dull ache and there is a pain in my chest. It hurts more when I breathe in. Those things aside, I feel remarkably well and I wonder again how long it has been since the ambush.

I pull back the sheet and ease my legs out of the bed. The floor is cool on my feet. There is no window, so I go to the door. It is locked. Of course. There is a window in the door and I peer through it, but I can see very little beyond that I am in a corridor and there is another door diagonally opposite to mine.

I go and sit on the bed. Nothing happens. I feel tired and lie back.

The next thing I know, I am waking up again.

I open my eyes. The ceiling is unchanged. There is a noise. Someone is in the room. I sit up quickly.

"Careful," says Sherman.

He is sitting on one of the two chairs. He puts his tab on the table. He is wearing his cadet uniform. There are scratches on his face, but they are fading.

"What happened?" I ask.

"Where should I start?"

I frown, trying to remember.

"Did I pull your father from that soft-top?"

"You did."

"Is he...okay?"

"He will be. His legs were shot up and he lost a fair bit of blood, but he didn't get shot again, or blown up by a grenade."

I nod.

"Thanks to you."

"To me?"

"You pulled him out of there. Another few seconds and he would have been caught in the blast from the grenades they tossed to finish us off."

I remember those last explosions now. So they were grenades.

"You took a few bullets yourself," he continues. "One in your shoulder, one through your lung, one in your leg, plus a few bits of shrapnel. Quite a collection."

"But I feel okay," I say. "How long have I been out?"

"Well the one in your shoulder was quite a tidy in and out. Just went through flesh. The one in your leg hit the bone. They had to pick bone fragments out and reattach the muscle and tendons. The lung was a bit serious, but they were able to patch that. And I suppose they just had to pick the shrapnel out of you. Same as they did for me."

He holds up his right arm.

"I got a bullet in this too. Doc says it'll be as good as new in a couple of weeks."

"How long have I been out?"

"Five days."

"Five days?"

"Well you came round occasionally. I've dropped in to see you a few times. We even had a conversation once. A bit of a weird one, I have to tell you, but I'll put that down to the drugs."

"No, I mean, I'm healing well for five days."

"I know. Cool isn't it?"

I lean back, puzzled. Something isn't making sense. I hate having this hole in my life.

"What about you?"

"Me?" He laughs ruefully. "I was just doing what a soldier does and firing back. We got one of them. And guess what? It was that big guy. The one from the forest."

"Double?"

"Yeah, that's what they called him wasn't it?"

I remember seeing the bigger man in the mask and thinking the way he moved was familiar. So it was Double. I liked him.

Then I remember the eyes of the man who shot me in the leg. I know now whose eyes they were. Rash.

"And Julius? Livia?"

"Your friends got away. All the rest of them got away."

He looks irritated. On the contrary, I am relieved. Julius has got away. I suppress a smile.

"How did it happen? How did they know the convoy was even there?"

Sherman shrugs.

"Scary huh?" he says. "Their intelligence must be extremely good. That's a worry. Their networks are better than we thought. Improving all the time."

There is silence.

"So what happens now?"

He smiles.

"That's the good bit. Well, one of them. You get to go home."

"Home?"

"Yeah. Home. Back to our place."

"But I'm under arrest."

"You were. But the Colonel is influential. And you were under his arrest anyway and not formally indicted into the penal system which also made things easier."

"I don't understand."

"My father is well aware of what you did for him. He was partly conscious at the time. And he saw what was left of the guard who was closer to the blast of the grenade. He asked me to tell you that you demonstrated your loyalty to the state during the ambush. You took bullets trying to save him."

That is not really how it was. He makes it sound as if I willingly took those bullets. I would rather not have been shot. I could have been killed. I didn't really think about the implications of what I was doing. I just saw the Colonel needed help.

"So I'm free?"

"Put it this way. You're no longer under arrest. And it gets better."

"Better?"

"Well you were pretty badly shot up. You had blood pouring out of you in multiple places and a ruptured lung. You weren't in good shape, but being a redblood, you weren't a priority."

"What do you mean? How is this better?"

"They had to deal with the Colonel first. No one knew what you'd done until he came around from his operation. Obviously they'd patched you up in triage. I made sure of that. But you'd lost a lot of blood and they don't carry plain blood in hospitals anymore and the Colonel was very grateful for what you did."

"What are you telling me?"

He looks me in the eyes and smiles broadly.

"They gave you nanomed blood."

"What?"

"Yeah, they gave you nanomed blood. You're a blueblood now."

How could they give me nanoblood? I try to make sense of this. It explains my rapid healing.

"So it's mine?"

"Yeah. The best reward there could be."

I'm speechless. One moment I'm on death row, the next I'm a hero. I'm struggling to take it all in.

The door opens and a doctor comes in. He has silver hair and a fleshless face.

"Good, you're awake," he says.

He marches over and takes my pulse. He shines a light in my eyes, then he puts a stethoscope to my chest. I'm unimpressed by his bedside manner, he didn't even ask. Then he inspects my wounds.

"Excuse me," I say. "I'm here too."

He looks at me with a frown.

"Quite the attitude for one so lucky," he says. "Few redbloods are accorded this honor."

I may have blueblood now, but I'm still thinking like a redblood. What is even more irritating is that he is still treating me like I'm a redblood.

"Well I have been. So I'm like you now," I say.

He looks at me disdainfully.

"You're not like me," he says. "You are a redblood with nanomeds."

He smiles a smile with closed lips. The only thing like a smile about it is that the corners of his mouth turn up. He glances at Sherman and nods at him, then leaves the room as abruptly as he came in.

Sherman smiles at me and shrugs.

This is my welcome to being a blueblood. I am still not accepted. They have become a race apart in their own minds.

I lie back and my mind turns to Julius and Livia who are out there somewhere, free. She is like me too now. Two new bluebloods. I wonder if she feels any different. I can't work out how I feel about it yet. It's too early.

"Doctor Menzies says he wants to keep you under observation for another week or so, then you'll need to come in from time to time," says Sherman.

"That seems like special attention."

"Well, you are special."

I almost shiver at how creepy that sounds.

"So you'd better get well soon," he continues. "Then you can come home."

"You said that before."

"Yeah. Back to the house. You're still a Hammond you know."

I was never a Hammond, but at least I have somewhere to go. It's what I've always wanted.

Sherman takes his leave and I'm left alone with my thoughts. I decide it is all too soon to think about this, so I turn on the live-stream. The images are of city streets, armored vehicles and Corps troopers. It turns out there has been a string of attacks across military targets in the city and other cities across the nation. We're all being warned to be on alert for terrorists, some of whom were killed by security forces.

It looks like the Rads are stepping things up. The government is talking about measures to isolate them, although they don't say what they are.

My mind turns to Julius again. Is he behind any of these attacks? I can see his eyes and his smile so clearly in my mind. I can't help but wonder if I will ever see him again. I shake my head. No, there is no chance of that. I am a blueblood now. I have had a lucky reprieve from the foolishness I got myself into.

I feel the wound in my shoulder again. My own nanomeds are working away inside me. I'm a blueblood.

So why do I feel uncomfortable?

***

Mouse returns in *Blue Blood Girl*.

Here's the book page on my website Blue Blood Girl - (kabarron.com)

She wants to live a new life, but they won't let her give up her old one.

Things are looking up for Mouse. She's got the nanobots, she's got a career, she's got a home with the Hammonds. But the Rads are becoming bolder, striking more and more often and making Mouse uneasy in her new skin.

When she bumps into a dangerous old acquaintance, she's asked to take risks with her new life, but something smells bad.

Then the government makes a shock announcement and one explosive night puts her new life in jeopardy. Can she persuade the Hammonds of her innocence? Can she even persuade herself? As the city dissolves into mayhem, she finds there's only one person she can trust. Herself.

Your free book is waiting

Pressed back into service as a fighter pilot when war breaks out, the man Mouse knows as Grandad meets a young girl in the rubble of a ruined city. It is a meeting which will change his life. And the lives of others he has yet to meet.

First Blood Girl provides context and insight to the unfolding story in the *Blood Girl* series.

Get a free digital copy of the prequel story *First Blood Girl* by tapping the image of the book above or on this sentence.

If you're reading a hard copy book with pages, you can use this link online: https://bit.ly/first-blood-girl

Enjoy this book? A few moments can help me

Honest reviews of my books help get them noticed by other readers. This is gold to an independent author like me.

If you've enjoyed this book, please take a few moments to leave a review at your favourite retailer. I know it's hard to write a review, but it can be as short as you like.

If you're reading this as an ebook:

Click here to leave a review on Amazon.com.

For Amazon.co.uk, this should get you there.

If you're not based in the US or UK, I apologise: neither am I. But I'd still appreciate a review if you could find your way to the right page.

Thank you for your time!

About the author

Usually to be found at the bottom of the world in New Zealand, and sometimes in his native Britain, Kevin is a writer, business consultant, improv performer and father.

Unable to keep to a single genre, his novels are currently science fiction and fantasy, but he also publishes travel, business and nonsense verse. There really aren't enough hours in the day, so he should just stop mucking about.

Find out more about KA Barron at www.kabarron.com.

Also by K.A. Barron

Science fiction and fantasy

Red Blood Girl

A safe life or a free life. She can't have both.

Fifty years after the war that destroyed civilization, the survivors have rebuilt inland away from the toxic coasts. The rich have nanomeds that keep them healthy. For the rest, an early death beckons.

Self-reliant and curious, Mouse grew up on the streets and made her own luck. Finding work as a domestic meant a home and security for Mouse in a military family with two brothers. One is charming, the other shuns her.

Shot down in a terrifying crash, Mouse meets the charismatic rebel leader Julius who wants nanotechnology for all. A single reckless decision sets in motion a train of events which turns her secure, reliable world upside down. Pursued by government forces, her need to protect herself is threatened by conflicting feelings of love, loyalty and guilt.

This is the first book in the *Blood Girl* series.

Blue Blood Girl

She wants to live a new life, but they won't let her give up her old one.

Things are looking up for Mouse. She's got the nanobots, she's got a career, she's got a home with the Hammonds. But the Rads are becoming bolder, striking more and more often and making Mouse uneasy in her new skin.

When she bumps into a dangerous old acquaintance, she's asked to take risks with her new life, but something smells bad.

Then the government makes a shock announcement and one explosive night puts her new life in jeopardy. Can she persuade the Hammonds of her innocence? Can she even persuade herself? As the city dissolves into mayhem, she finds there's only one person she can trust. Herself.

Blue Blood Girl is the second book in the Blood Girl series.

Light Funnel

A father in despair. An ancient destiny. A darkness that changes everything.

Richard is out of work, depressed and shutting out his young son Charlie. Then, unwittingly transported through their dreams to a new world, they find themselves on opposite sides in a centuries old conflict. In the mage lands of this alien world, lost crusaders battle the Delf who can create wraiths of fire.

But when war begins, Richard finds his arrival has unleashed a nightmare from the past which threatens to consume both worlds.

As darkness pours from the earth and armies gather, Charlie and his father discover that there are horrors in the darkness of dreams which will take them further and further from home.

Light Funnel is the first in a series of dark epic fantasy novels set in parallel worlds.

Light Needle

In dreams, something is stirring.

Eight years have passed since the events described in Light Funnel. An uneasy peace has existed between the Order and the Delf. Now, rumblings of dissent threaten a return to war.

Inspired by dreams, Jack Silver searches for the descendants of the adventurers who left Outreterre centuries before and never returned. With their help, the Delf could be overthrown forever.

Former adversaries Berwick, Rodon and Raul secretly follow Silver and his protectors across the sea; Solimo, still haunted by his experiences, is about to face his greatest fear, while a footloose Charlie Denham will soon be fleeing for his life from forces he does not understand.

For an old enemy will stop at nothing to purge the worlds. A great city will burn and a society will be torn apart. Only a fragile web of alliances, old and new, stands before the terrible new power emerging from Limbo.

In this second book in the *Light Funnel* series, multiple storylines weave together culminating in a climactic confrontation.

Travel and humour

Into the blue: Half-planned travels of an amateur vagabond

Kevin Barron feels guilty if he stays at home and does nothing. His solution is to visit other countries and do nothing there instead. An added benefit is that writing about it gives him something to do at home.

Lose your ticket before you've even set off, find out what whalers think of Greenpeace, dodge dive-bombers, meet dangerous truckers, interview a tennis star, witness horror, walk all night, fish for your dinner, watch sunsets in the wilderness, ride legendary highways, stargaze in the Rockies, hitch-hike through the outback, be rescued by an angel, become Robin Hood, escape from Colditz.

This collection of stories covers more than a decade of travel, so throw your backpack over your shoulder and head off...into the blue.

Not there yet: Wandering home with an amateur vagabond

When you leave, at what point do you start going home? And when you leave and don't come back, where is home?

Moving to another country for a while provides an excellent opportunity to travel on the way. Having threatened The Big Trip for years,

Kevin Barron finally takes the plunge and, as a result, finds that the idea of home is not as clear as it used to be.
Kayak in the rain, meet an Aboriginal elder, make conversation with a grumpy barber, kill sheep, crash a car, eat entrails, be in the Middle East on 9/11, ride legendary highways, find yourself face to face with an elk, get lost in the African night, have the best view at Shangri-La, fight a fire, be ill on an overnight bus, search for intruders, flirt, haggle, dance, joke, eat, hike, misunderstand, leave home and return.

These stories follow those of *Into the Blue*, so throw your backpack over your shoulder again and set off on the never-ending journey home.

Tales of Socks and Splendour

The Grumpete is a disgusting yet warm hearted character who lives alone in a land beyond the Ocean of Spleg. Embarking on an adventure one day, he encounters the Kazza Princess in a distant castle and their lives are never the same again.
Join the foul-bummed Grumpete and the kimmering Kazz as they shine, explode, wander, flatulate, burn, run, reproduce, eat and fight their way through a series of far-fetched adventures in glorious nonsense verse.
Whether read out loud or quietly to yourself where no one will find you, these fast-moving and humorous poems are sure to entertain children of all ages...apart from perhaps those of a delicate disposition.

Business

How to Run Facilitated Workshops: a pragmatic guide to successful meetings

Are your meetings a waste of time? Get productive.

We've all had those moments when you wonder what the point is of getting together at work. People wander off topic, take over, tune out... In today's fast moving business environment, you need to make the most of people's time, energy and knowledge.

This book is packed full of advice and techniques to help you prepare for, run and follow up on facilitated workshops. Not only is the process described, but there is advice for dealing with problems along the way, notably managing behavior that can kill productivity and collaboration. There is a focus on planning the workshop and setting out the agenda. A set of sample agendas covering a wide range of project scenarios is included.

With the advice in this book, gleaned from twenty years of experience in industry and consulting, you can pre-empt problems and be well on the way to saving time and achieving usable outcomes that will accelerate your projects.

www.ingramcontent.com/pod-product-compliance
Lightning Source LLC
LaVergne TN
LVHW091140080826
845145LV00008B/2213

* 9 7 8 1 9 9 1 1 7 5 3 1 1 *